T0354591

A. DRAGONBLOOD

LEAVING
SHAD⊕WS

CHILDREN OF THE OTHERS
COLLECTION™ BOOK - FOUR

LEAVING SHADOWS

CHILDREN OF THE OTHERS COLLECTION - BOOK FOUR

A. DRAGONBLOOD
COVER BY TED KAY

authorHOUSE®

AuthorHouse™
1663 Liberty Drive
Bloomington, IN 47403
www.authorhouse.com
Phone: 1-800-839-8640

© 2012 A. Dragonblood. All rights reserved.

No part of this book may be reproduced, stored
in a retrieval system, or transmitted by any means
without the written permission of the author.

First published by AuthorHouse 10/3/2012

ISBN: 978-1-4772-7383-8 (sc)
ISBN: 978-1-4772-7382-1 (e)

Library of Congress Control Number: 2012917787

Printed in the United States of America

Any people depicted in stock imagery provided
by Thinkstock are models, and such images are
being used for illustrative purposes only.
Certain stock imagery © Thinkstock.

This book is printed on acid-free paper.

Because of the dynamic nature of the Internet, any web
addresses or links contained in this book may have changed
since publication and may no longer be valid. The views
expressed in this work are solely those of the author and do
not necessarily reflect the views of the publisher, and the
publisher hereby disclaims any responsibility for them.

This book is dedicated to
Mom

ACKNOWLEDGEMENTS

My readers respectively know as "The Others or The Ones" I thank you for sharing in this story with your encouragement online, at book signings, school visits and sharing it with your friends. You have given me the confidence to continue writing my own stories and I have plenty of them.

To my beautiful and genius wife who knows me best, whose belief and encouragement is more that any husband or author could ask. Your ability to listen when I feel I am lost always guides me back to the path.

To my son who keeps track of time for me when I am lost in the world of writing, making sure that I am never later for a meeting, dinner or a game. You continue to inspire me as I watch you grow up so fast, often wanting to slow you down just so I don't miss anything.

To my friends that continue to inform me that I am a little delusional and disturbed, you remind me that I am doing exactly what I meant too.

To my sanctuary where I always feel safe to read and write anything and everything that has created a reality in my head.

CHAPTER ONE

UNDERCOVER TROUBLE

Vampires littered the roof tops and wolves lurked in the shadows of doorways and alleys as the three girls started home. They gripped each other's hands as tightly as their spandex tops embraced their young female bodies. They were scurrying home from the movie theatre after an evening showing of 'The Vampire's Spawn.' The night was eerily quiet when they crossed the theatre's empty parking lot. The movie hadn't been particularly good and they hadn't told their parents where they were going, so no one knew they were there. At least, that is what they thought.

It had all started with some hot guys from school that were giving out free tickets to some of the girls. Katelyn thought it would be a cool thing to go check out the movie, hoping that the guys would be there and she could maybe hook up with one of them. Smart enough to not go alone, she instructed Tori and Jenny to come along but tell their parents that they were staying at her house for the night.

None of the girls could actually see the vampires. They melted into the night sky where it draped the tops of the city's architecture with shadows. They could hear the rustling of clothes and high pitched whining. The girls' tanned arms were now speckled white with goose bumps from their innate sense of danger. They hurried down the street, a fast walk turning into a run as the noises became more distinct.

"Do you see what's up there?" Tori asked the others.

"I don't know what's up but I keep seeing something out of the corner of my eye in every store front," Jenny replied, shaking."This way." Katelyn motioned with her free hand as she pointed to a one way street that was poorly lit by only one street light. "There are still three or four houses down there. We are better off on a residential street than a commercial road where everything is closed," she explained.

2

The other two girls were not as familiar as Katelyn was with the area, so they followed her lead. Exhausted from running six blocks in sandals, the young women slowed their pace. They tried to slow their heart rates too, so they could hear from where their pursuers were coming.

"Maybe we lost them," Jenny suggested, wishing she was right.

"You may be right, but we should still be careful and stay close," Tori stated.

The three let go of each other's hands, wiping off the buttery sweat that they had collected from nerves and popcorn.

"Did you feel that?" Katelyn asked her friends.

"Feel what?" Jenny asked Katelyn looking in her direction.

"I thought I felt something breeze by my face."

Tori turned and looked at Katelyn. "I think you must have run into something. There's blood on the side of your cheek."

"OMG!" Katelyn screamed as she dragged her hand over the seeping wound. "It's just like the vampires in the movie. They teased and played with their victims before they drained them!"

"Let's not get too dramatic, Katelyn," Jenny advised. "I mean, this is not a movie. That stuff is just fiction and urban legends anyway," she added.

"Well to be honest, every story has to have a beginning. I for one believe that there are real vampires. I mean like human vampires, not the movie superhero, super-lover ones. Of course, if they have super powers and are super lovers that would be a bonus!" Tori giggled nervously.

"Well, this blood seeping from my face is very real and I am really scared. We are still five blocks from home," Katelyn whimpered.

"Come on, let's see if someone can help us and get you cleaned up," Jenny suggested.

While the three frightened young women approached each house to look for help, the vampires and wolves were up to their own games. Free falling from the top of one house, one of the vampires landed softly on his feet and blended into the shadows. A large four-legged beast appeared abruptly beside him.

"They are ours tonight," the vampire declared.

"Jonathan, you know that it is first come, first serve when it comes to such tasty little treats as these three young humans," the wolf replied.

"Sebastian, we were the ones that planted the free tickets in the hands of this girl. Why should we do all the work and you feast?" Jonathan demanded.

Their stares stretched timelessly, broken only when Sebastian raised his heavy paw towards Jonathan's face. Jonathan had already detected the blood trail that Katelyn was leaving on the sidewalk. He was anxious to taste it, fresh from her vein. Knowing that it was Sebastian that had had the first taste made Jonathan's own blood boil. His jaw line dropped, his fangs extended from his gum line, and his hands buckled and cracked as talons pierced through his knuckles. He raised his head and his eyes had been replaced by black orbs of simmering anger.

"If it was a game you wanted tonight, you should have just said so," Jonathan growled to Sebastian. "Game On!"

Like cool breeze on a warm summer night, the rest of the vampires launched themselves from the roof tops, lunging at the wolf beasts. All of them were heading towards the three young women who were now at the last house on the street, hoping that someone was home to assist them.

"Hello, Hello is anyone there? Please, open the door; we need your help!" Jenny cried as she rang the door bell repeatedly.

There was a crash inside the house, sounding like someone had knocked over a table or broken some dishes. They pounded on the door again. Behind them they could hear growling. Almost too scared to look, the girls turned around. Two huge wolves sat at the bottom of the stairs growling at them. Racing across the street were two pretty good looking guys, with the exception of their fangs and hollowed out eyes.

Katelyn kept repeating, "This isn't real, this isn't real, this isn't real."

The door to the house flew open and the girls hurled themselves into the front hallway, slamming the door behind them. They didn't hear anything, thinking maybe they were safe. But who opened the door and whose house were they in?

"Are they gone? Is anybody there?" Jenny whispered in the dim lit room.

"Quiet, I heard something in there." Tori

pointed to the back sitting room. "Follow me and stay close."

Jenny grabbed Tori's hand and reached to where Katelyn was a few moments ago to take her hand. She wasn't there.

"Tori, where is Katelyn?" Jenny screamed hysterically.

"Calm down, it's pretty dark in here. Maybe she walked that way," Tori replied reassuringly.

The two girls opened the curtained doors to the sitting room. They stepped cautiously into the room. Suddenly, the door slammed behind them and the room lit up with candles. There was a fine mist engulfing the room like an early morning fog.

"Welcome to my home, ladies," a voice announced. The fine mist slowly began to dissipate.

The girls gasped as they saw half a dozen men and women, all dressed in black with hollowed out eyes, circling them. The circle parted and a tall, slender man, not much older than a teen ager himself, entered the circle with Katelyn limp in his arms. Her eyes were clouded over, her face withdrawn and pale.

"Katelyn! Who are you and what have you down to our friend?" Tori demanded.

One of the vampire women grabbed Tori by the arm and pulled her away from the man.

"Let her go, my darling. She won't harm me. I am Jonathan the Vampire Prince," the man announced, while his minions lowered their heads to him.

"Mmmmmm, I do apologize for all the drama this evening," he continued in a melodic voice. "Sometimes the wolves like to play their petty games with us. I suppose it adds another dimension of thrill to the kill." Jonathan chuckled and cradled Katelyn to his chest.

"So, here we are. This one is exactly where I wanted her, when I gave her tickets to the movie. You two are a little extra bonus that I wasn't counting on, so I decided to invite a few friends over to enjoy an early evening snack with me!" The other vampires joined the siren call of his laughter and the circle started to shrink.

Gathering her strength, Tori smiled back at Jonathan and began to clap her hands, lightly at first and then with a more pounding rhythm.

"This is why I thought that vampire movie was lame, and why I feel that many of the vampire books and stories are so dumb," Tori announced.

Silence fell on the crowd of vampires. Jenny clung more tightly to Tori's hand.

"Here you are - big, bad vampire guy preying on silly teen age girls that couldn't fight back against you if they tried. You are no better or different than the bullies that we go to school with or the child molesters, rapists or killers in mainstream society," Tori blurted, still looking around the room for any possible way out.

Jonathan laid Katelyn in a nearby chair. He cracked his knuckles and straightened his shirt by tucking the tail back into his pants. Then he released his fangs. "Shut up the stinking wolves," he ordered one of the other vampires. "They are still causing a commotion out on the porch. And make sure the lock is on the door, too," he reminded his less-than-ambitious assistant.

"So then my dear little girl," he continued smoothly, "I suppose it would be safe to say that you probably didn't believe in vampires or werewolves until tonight either." Jonathan walked slowly around the group of vampires in attendance.

"WELL DID YOU OR DIDN'T YOU? ANSWER

ME!" Jonathan snarled, upset and losing patience with the situation.

"Ah, um excuse me vampire prince sir," Jenny interrupted. "Tori was the only one who did believe that vampires were real. She just didn't think you were like this. She thought that you were smart and magical - like demigods that were here to keep order and ensure that stories were kept and people were protected from their foolishness. She thought that vampires were pretty hot, too."

Tori smiled at her friend and started backing towards the door ever so slightly. Meanwhile Jonathan and the other vampires had begun to chatter among themselves about what Jenny had said.

"Well, I must say that may have been true a hundred to three thousand years ago," Jonathan replied. "But people are living longer, and Wikipedia, Google and everyone's personal website record histories, so we have had to evolve to survive," Jonathan explained.

"I am sorry that you have fallen into the myths of this world, truly I am. But you can't go around scaring and killing people just because you can't find your place in this new world. I think you have become quite short sighted," Tori replied.

Jonathan turned and looked at their friend lying on the chair. He got down on one knee and placed her hand on his face.

"She wanted me, whether I was a vampire or not. So I do not think that any changes are needed." He turned back around to see his followers nodding their agreement, but the girls were not there.

"There they are, at the door, stop them!" he bellowed as Tori flung the door open and hid behind it just as the wolves pounced through the door.

The shrieks from inside the house were so loud that both girls had to cover their ears to muffle the sounds of terror.

"Ethan, Ethan, ETHAN!" Helen pulled back the covers shrouding Ethan and the book he was reading in bed.

"I don't know what it is that you are reading, but give it here, now!" Ethan's mother was not happy at all. "<u>The Vampire Prince</u>," she said, reading the cover of the book.

She shook her head. "Where did you get this trash?" she demanded.

Ethan regularly read under the covers,

since he was never tired when he had to go to bed. His mom had never come barging into his room and pulled the covers off before, though. He realized he must have been broadcasting strong emotions. He had become agitated at the way the vampire prince was handling things. The poor girls were probably going to die.

"Sorry Mom," Ethan answered guiltily. "I was just curious about a book that a lot of kids in school were reading about vampires. I wanted to read it to see how real it was." He added, "I am not enjoying it very much."

"What is going on in here?" Ethan's father asked as he walked in the room.

Helen handed Atticus the book.

"<u>The Vampire Prince</u> - is it a biography or fiction?" Atticus asked Ethan.

Looking a little stumped, Ethan replied "I hope it is fiction, Father; these vampires are really mean to the humans and the wolves and each other."

Smiling at Ethan, his father said, "You know that we can all be mean to one another. Perhaps you have that figured out already. I can see that your energy must have alarmed your mother, causing her to come in here quite upset." Atticus placed a hand on his wife's shoulder.

"I was getting angry with the vampires in the story; I guess that is what Mom felt. I am sorry Mom, I won't do it again." Ethan leaned over and hugged her tightly.

"I am sure that there will be other times that you will get your mother worried. We haven't even hit the teen years yet. But I am pleased that you understand that this is not an appropriate book for you," Ethan's father observed.

"Now I think you need to get some sleep, whether you are tired or not. Good night, son." Atticus gave him a kiss on the forehead.

"I will be going to bed shortly myself, but first I want a few words with Ethan," Helen told her husband as he left. Atticus nodded and returned to his study.

"I am really sorry Mom. I know that it is a teen book and I am not supposed to be reading it, but I was curious. How am I supposed to discuss it with others if I don't know what they are talking about?" Ethan hoped his explanation would keep him out of trouble for not telling her in the first place.

Helen recognized his negotiating and did

understand his reasoning. But what he had experienced while reading worried her.

"This is definitely one of those times when you were better off asking forgiveness than permission," she admitted. "I could feel your anger and frustration, Ethan. You were disturbed and upset. I am proud of you for knowing the difference between what is necessary and what is wrong, but I thought you were being tormented in your sleep."

As Helen got up, Ethan asked, "Can I finish the book? I only have two chapters left. Please?"

"No, you don't need to read this nonsense," she replied firmly.

"How am I going to know what happened in the end of the book?" Ethan pleaded.

Helen turned out his light and with the dim hall light behind her she said, "The wolves and vampires fight, no one really wins but the girls sneak out from behind the door. Jenny runs out the door while Tori heads back into the room to survey the damages. She sees her friend dead on the chair, while the vampire prince struggles to stay alive. Tori makes him look into her eyes and says 'you give us all a bad name, and for that you don't deserve to live.'

"She reaches down, pulls his head up to her and plunges her razor sharp fangs into his throat, draining him of any life that remains. She drops him on the floor, picks up the lone candle on the entrance table and throws it into the nest of bodies and debris and walks out of the house. The house explodes and the bodies of her friend, the vampires and wolves burn in a horrific fire, a house party that went terribly wrong. The end."

"Seriously Mom, is that how it ends?" Ethan asks after a minute.

"Maybe it did, or maybe that is the way it should have ended, with dumb girls and bad vampires. I guess you will never know. I also know that it was Gabriel who loaned you this book. I will keep it until I see him again. Good night!"

CHAPTER TWO

TOO EARLY FOR SOME

It was early on a Saturday morning in late April; too early after the events of the night before. Ethan was still not sure if his mother told him the true ending to the book. He wasn't bringing it up, though; better to leave it alone.

Ethan watched the night become day as his mother drove him into town. He was heading to Jeremy's house to spend the weekend.

"Mom, did you see them?" Ethan asked. He had noticed a large cluster of shadowy people swarm on the side of the road.

"I didn't see them, but I felt them. They are probably trying to get home before the sun comes up, in which case they better hurry," she replied.

His mother had to work all weekend at her lab. She was not comfortable leaving

Ethan alone, even with the protection they had around their house. She joked with Ethan that it wasn't him she was worried about, but what he would do to someone who did try anything. Teasing aside, she was honestly scared at what he was capable of doing. His new preteen hormones presented an extra challenge in matters of control.

His father was home, but spending more time at the manufacturing plant. They were expanding local operations for a new generation of solar cells. He was trying to have everything on line before Ethan's summer break, so this year they could take a family vacation. Atticus had missed most of the past few years pursuing the mirror men.

"Remember, Jeremy and his family are not morning people," Ethan's mother reminded him as they arrived at Senona and Luis' house. "Senona said that she would have Luis leave the front door unlocked when he left for work, so just walk in and go straight to Jeremy's room," she added.

"I got it Mom, don't worry. The last thing I want to do is wake up Ms. Senora on a Saturday morning. Jeremy has told me how she is if she doesn't get her beauty sleep; she turns into a wicked witch! You would think that it would be us that would be horrible morning people, based on T.V. and movie vampires," Ethan replied.

"It is a good thing that we don't follow the code of the script writers and media or we would miss out on half the day," Helen responded. "Please don't get into any trouble! Don't forget to brush your teeth and I will see you tomorrow night."

"Really Mom, do you have to remind me every time to brush my teeth? I will try to remember," Ethan replied, shaking his head as he closed the car door behind him. He thought, so which is it - don't get in any trouble, brush your teeth or all of the above?

"All of the above!" his mom replied, now shaking her head. Ethan turned and smiled, then started up the front stairs.

The huge lead glass door creaked on its hinges and seemed to close itself behind Ethan as he entered the foyer of Jeremy's old house. The inside had been restored beautifully by Jeremy's dad to its original grandeur, but with many modern conveniences. Ethan heard a low snap like the breaking of a small branch. It was the oversized brass deadbolt lock setting itself again now that he had arrived.

Ethan took a deep breath and started down the hallway towards Jeremy's room. It was still dark in the closed house, eerily quiet and even a little spooky for a spring morning. His nerves tingled, like when he was watching a scary movie on T.V. and didn't know what was going to happen next.

Closing his eyes, Ethan made his way down the hallway ever so carefully as not to disturb Ms. Senona. He didn't really care if Jeremy or Max woke up; after all, what was he going to do in Jeremy's room until he got up anyway?

He made the final turn to Jeremy's room. Soundlessly he opened Jeremy's door and something hard fell on his head.

"Ah, what the...!" Ethan squealed and bit his tongue, trying not to yell from the pain of a marble-based soccer trophy landing in the center of his skull.

Covering his face with a pillow trying not to laugh, Jeremy sat up in his bed and threw a pillow at his friend.

"I knew you were trying that stealth mode thing you do," Jeremy said. "If you would have opened your eyes when you opened the door, you would have caught my trophy trap. Unless your vampire reflexes aren't as fast as my garg-witch moves," Jeremy teased, jumping up out of his bed and prancing around like some crazed MMA prize fighter.

Ethan ducked out of the way of a few of his friend's moves. He motioned a few punches back and then grappled him into a head lock.

"Really Jeremy, you knew I was going to be here early and you still had to set a trap on the door?" Ethan asked.

"You can't be too careful these days, you know," Jeremy replied, slipping out of Ethan's grasp.

"If I was a bad guy and I made it through the front door or any other entrance in your house, I think I would be too scared to go any further. I don't know why I always get freaked out when I walk through your house alone," Ethan added.

"You get used to it. This house is really old. People have died in it and my mom likes to use that energy to strengthen her spells," a little voice said from under the bed.

"Is that you Max?" Ethan asked.

Ethan knew it was Max under the bed, but it was a game they had been playing for a while, where Max tried to surprise Ethan.

"I told you that you can't hide from Ethan.

No human can hide from a vampire, especially a young vampire," Jeremy explained, looking under the bed at Max.

"Good morning Ethan," Max announced as he slid out from under the bed.

"Jeremy let me sleep in his room last night so I could see you early. You know boy talk and that very important stuff girls can't hear."

"Hey, I let you sleep in my room so that you wouldn't snitch on me," Jeremy reminded him.

"What is it now?" Ethan asked Jeremy. "Did you put a hole in the ceiling, crush the door handle, make a new designer scent that smells like skunk or – no, don't tell me - you broke the toilet again?" Ethan suggested, laughing.

"None of the above," Jeremy replied. "I have better control than that over my gifts."

Max looked at the floor and laughed loud enough that Jeremy punched his shoulder.

"Don't hit your brother like that, Jeremy. What did Max do to you?" Ethan punched Jeremy back on Max's behalf.

"He laughed at your jokes about me," Jeremy retorted.

"That is because they were funny, and

because you really did those things," Ethan commented.

"Sorry little bro, I shouldn't have hit you." Jeremy shrugged sheepishly.

"So what is it that you did that Max is hiding from I assume your mom and dad?"

Ethan asked again.

"Well it is kind of a long story but I will try to give you the short version," Jeremy replied.

If there is one thing that a witch can't do, it's give a short version of anything, Ethan thought to himself. He was known to be a bit of a bard himself, but witches - they didn't like to miss a single detail. Their stories were passed down this way throughout the centuries. Many witches felt safer with oral histories, since anything written could become incriminating in the wrong hands. Ethan's father felt that way about texting or emailing others in the community, but in business he wrote everything down. Ethan decided he should sit down for this explanation.

"Ok, well it all started three weeks ago when I was trying to get some homework finished in class. This girl in my class, Callie, started poking me with her pencil. When

I ignored her, she threw little notes at me which she insisted I read."

"Callie, why haven't I heard of Callie before?" Ethan interrupted.

"She loves Jeremy!" Max yelped.

Jeremy was thinking of punching Max again but he knew that he was right. Besides, Ethan would make him apologize again.

"Ok, maybe she likes me a little, but love? I don't think so," Jeremy replied.

"Well do you like her too?" Ethan asked.

Jeremy hesitated, so Ethan knew that Jeremy liked her some even if he denied it.

"Nah, not really. I mean she is pretty fine, but she is so pushy and touchy and yappy. You understand, right?" Jeremy asked Ethan.

Ethan, who was still younger than Jeremy and Camille, liked the girls in his class. He would joke with them and play sports with them, but had no real interest in them otherwise.

Ethan replied, "Well, I have friends that are girls, like Camille and Gretchen. But I don't really think I have had enough experience with them to comment."

"When you talk like that, I am reminded that you are a vampire. You are always so diplomatic and clever with your words," Jeremy commented.

"Anyway, back to the story. So Callie walks up to our teacher Ms. Longtuths' desk to ask her a question and on her way back to her seat she knocks my book off my desk to get my attention. As I reached down to pick it up, she reached down at the same time and banged her head into mine. I should have laughed, but instead I blurted out for her to stop messing with me.

"Ms. Longtuth jumped out of her chair like it was a fire drill and headed in our direction, all the while yelling at me like it was my fault. Callie was now crying, even though she wasn't crying 10 seconds earlier. Next thing I know she is signing for me to go to the headmaster's office while walking Callie to the nurse's room. Now it was my parents that were being called to the school to discuss my anger issues and problem with authority."

There was silence for a few minutes as Jeremy regained his composure and Ethan tried to figure out why Jeremy was the one getting in trouble.

"Tell Ethan what else happened," Max added.

Ever since their experiences in the Asylum

last year, Max had become more outgoing. He still had many autistic characteristics, but he wasn't as shy with other children. In fact, that St. Patrick's Day had changed all of them. Jeremy struggled equally with puberty and his temper. Camille kept her distance as her coming of age ritual loomed closer. Gretchen stayed more out than in, aggravating her dads mercilessly. Mercy had landed a real job after Senona had introduced her to a fashion designer she had met writing an article about steam punk. Ethan was extremely focused on his schoolwork, trying to wrap his 12 year old brain around as much as possible.

"So what is it you are not telling me?" Ethan asked. "You know that I could find out if you don't tell me out loud."

They had promised not to use their gifts on each other unless necessary. Jeremy doubted that Ethan would follow through on his threat of reading his mind, but he knew that Ethan would understand what happened if he filled in the blanks.

"Alright," Jeremy sighed, looking at Max with one eyebrow cocked. "While Ms. Longtuth was yelling at ME, and everyone else put their heads down on their desks, I kind of used magic."

"You kind of used magic? You don't kind of use magic, you either cast it or you don't," Ethan exclaimed.

"Alright, I used it. You make me sound like I'm a drug addict or something!"

"Magic can be like a drug. Mommy always tells us that, Jeremy," Max added.

Jeremy knew that Max was right. His family had had many issues in the past with magic abuse. It wasn't really until his mom's generation that they improve their control.

"Ms. Longtuth's yelling was hurting my ears and Callie's crying wasn't helping. So I cast the 'croak in the throat' spell - just a little spell, with no real side effects. I was this close to garging out, right there in class. That would have been worse I think, but I controlled the urge," Jeremy reasoned.

Ethan laughed.

"What's so funny? I am the one having to write 5000 lines, and I was minding my own business," Jeremy demanded.

Ethan had to write lines sometimes as punishment, and he knew writing 5000 lines was not funny. Jeremy was too old to spank, which wouldn't hurt his gargoyle butt anyway. Being grounded in his room just gave him time to make designer spells while rearranging furniture. He didn't care about phones or computer stuff. Writing lines was definitely the worst punishment for Jeremy, because he couldn't do anything else but write and he had to see, read and write the same words over and over and over again.

"I am not laughing about writing lines; I hate writing lines," Ethan replied. "It's the 'croak in the throat'. Where do you come up with these names for spells?"

Jeremy pondered the question. 'Croak in the throat' didn't seem weird to him. Obviously the name described taking away the ability of speech without using candles, herbs or long incantations.

"I don't know, they are just what we are taught. They are like hundreds of years old from the old country, so I guess that was the way it was translated," Jeremy replied defensively.

"So let me get this straight, you did the 'croak in the throat' spell and both the teacher and Callie lost their voices. If no one knows that you cast, though, how did you get in trouble?" Ethan asked.

"Only Ms. Longtuth lost her voice and that was just for a few hours. The class started laughing at her because she sounded like she had a frog in her throat. That made her embarrassed and even madder at me. Then I argued with her about what happened and she couldn't talk back. When my mom got to the school and the headmaster had to interpret for Ms. Longtuth, I knew I was in big trouble," Jeremy explained.

"Yeah, you really did get yourself in more trouble than necessary," Ethan agreed. "I mean, it wasn't your fault, but when it is your word against a teacher, you're doomed! I am guessing you are in trouble for using magic again in school?"

"Yeah, I should have just stopped while I was ahead. It's hard for me to make those decisions quickly. I mean, regular quotidian kids can't think that fast since their frontal lobe isn't developed. Expecting us to not accidentally use our gifts when provoked is ridiculous," Jeremy complained.

Ethan and Max sat perplexed on the side of the bed. The frontal lobe and quotidian kids must be from some SyFy show that Jeremy watched.

"What? Why are you guys looking at me like that?" Jeremy asked.

"You kind of lost me when you were talking

about the lobe thing and then the quotidian kids," Ethan replied.

Jeremy smiled, remembering that he was older and probably wiser too.

"The frontal lobe is part of your brain. My mom keeps reminding herself that is why I don't always think things out first," Jeremy explained.

Ethan interrupted, "Should we be worried that you are missing part of your brain?"

"No, it is not like that," Jeremy corrected him. "Your frontal lobe is the part of the brain that makes decisions and stuff like that. It doesn't really develop until we are older, like 20 or something, unless we exercise it."

Ethan shrugged. "Then who or what are quotidians?"

"Mercy had been talking to Camille about what her generation called the ordinary kids, the ones that didn't want to develop their gifts or didn't have any. Mercy's generation called them the mundane and the generation before that called them the norms, but Camille thought it would be a good idea to amp up the name a little," Jeremy explained. "She asked us to use 'quotidian' for a few months and see if it worked."

Ethan and Max shrugged again, uninterested.

"So you have to write 5000 lines, that's steep!" Ethan changed the subject. "What does it say and what number are you at right now?"

Jeremy replied, "*I will work on my control issues and not use magic in school.*"

"Are you going to have to do that all day?" Ethan asked. "We won't be able to play or go to the cave to use the punching bag and stuff."

"I should be finished in around an hour," Jeremy replied, using the tone of voice that always ended with them running, hiding or pleading.

"Whatever you are up to must be why Max got to stay in your room all night. Keeping him quiet keeps you from getting in more trouble," Ethan observed.

"Yeah, something like that," Jeremy agreed as he opened the door to the cave.

The three boys made their way down to Jeremy's secret space where they found Spartan laying at the bottom of the stairs.

Ethan figured that he was guarding the space.

He reached down and gave the dog a few

strokes, saying "I wondered where you were. Someday I am going to be able to feel your energy, even in secret spaces."

Spartan rolled over long enough for Max to rub his belly, then he was back to sleep.

On an old desk in the corner of the dark room there was a candle burning. As Ethan approached the desk he could see a feather pen moving back and forth across a stack of papers. When he moved closer, he saw the pen was busy writing Jeremy's lines, *'I will work on my control issues and not use magic in school'.*

"If your mom finds out, you are going to be in even more trouble." Ethan warned Jeremy. "Besides, I see two problems," Ethan added.

"What?!" Jeremy growled.

"First, how do you know how many lines you have not really written?" Ethan asked.

"That isn't a problem," Jeremy assured him. "There are 33 lines per page, so 66 lines front and back, since my parents won't let me waste paper. I worked it out. I have to complete 76 pages in total, which I worked into the incantation. So what is the second problem?"

"You are missing the word 'not' in every

sentence and it looks like you are through over 60 pages," Ethan pointed out.

"No way, it can't be!" Jeremy shouted, jumping up from the sofa. He cringed at the thought of how the sentence would read if it was missing the word 'not.'"

He raced to the desk, ready to break the spell, when Ethan and Max started laughing. Jeremy realized that Ethan was teasing and no words were missing. He turned and dove onto the sofa and tackled Ethan.

"You just about gave me a garg-out moment. I'm going to use our 'croak in throat' spell on you," Jeremy said as he landed.

> You have insulted me and
> did me wrong
>
> Now a frog shall sit where your
> voice belongs

"Jeremy, dear, I know that you are down there writing your lines. Are Ethan and Max with you?" Jeremy's mom yelled down the stairs.

Clearing his throat, Ethan replied, "Yes, Ms. Senona I am down here with Jeremy and Max. I am sorry if we woke you up too early Madame," he added.

"No, you boys didn't wake me up. It was time for me to rise and capture the day. Will you and Max take Spartan outside, please?" she asked. "Jeremy needs to keep working on his lines if he wants to have any fun today."

"Yes, right away," Ethan replied as he wiggled free from Jeremy's hold.

"Apparently you can't use 'croak throat' on me," Ethan snickered. "You did, however, almost choke me to death so I guess that would be called the 'choke throat' spell." Ethan ran up the stairs before Jeremy could grab him again.

"At least I don't have to walk Spartan when I am grounded," Jeremy called after them smugly.

CHAPTER THREE

WALK A BLOCK

E than and Max walked around four blocks and two parks before Spartan finally did his business. Ethan was a little surprised at how far they were allowed to walk Spartan without adult supervision. However, Ethan appreciated the one on one time with Max. They talked about his school year, which was coming to an end in a few weeks, as well as how his training was developing.

Even though Max was a few years younger than Ethan, he was not shy about sharing his experiences.

"School has been good. I like my teachers but I don't really like all the kids that I have in my classes. Some are very mean and I really mean, mean!" Max said emphatically.

"I am sorry they are mean to you, Max. Do

you think they are mean on purpose or do they not know any different?" Ethan asked.

Ethan had talked more with his mother and Ms. Senona about autism since he found out that Max had this condition.

Some kids could learn to manage their condition to appear almost unaffected. Others still struggled and could seem very distant, distracted or even mean. Ethan knew that Max's family and community worked with him all the time. They had special diets, careful teachings of both magic and regular routines, as well as constant attention to the direction of his development.

Max thought about what Ethan asked him and replied, "I think it is both, but it makes me sad if some kids don't understand that I am not a freak."

FREAK was a word that Ethan didn't like and his father hated that word even more.

"You are certainly not a freak, Max. If anything you are more gifted than all of us because you can clearly feel and see everything without preconceptions," Ethan reassured him.

Max gave Ethan a hug and replied, "I know. You are not a freak either. You are my best vampire friend in the world. Am I your friend too?" Max wanted to make sure he could be friends with Jeremy's best friend.

"Duh, yes of course you are my friend too!" Ethan replied.

They continued to walk along the quiet morning street when Max blurted out, "Jeremy is always getting in trouble with his magic. He needs to be more careful. Mom and Dad are worried that he will get caught or hurt himself or someone else."

"I hear what you are saying Max but I think that Jeremy has more control than we think he does. He just likes to play the tough guy when really he is pretty careful," Ethan said thoughtfully.

"Don't tell Jeremy but I got in trouble last night too," Ethan continued.

"What did you do?" Max asked, perplexed.

"I snuck a book into the house to read. It was a vampire book for older kids, like teenagers. Everyone is reading it so I wanted to read it too. I mean I should know what vampires do in teen books, right?" Ethan asked rhetorically. "But I got caught by my mom and we had to have a talk about it."

"Was it a nasty book like my mom calls them?" Max asked.

"I don't know about nasty, but it was

weird. I mean weird in the sense that the vampires are always portrayed as bad guys or predators. I am not saying that we can't be predators sometimes but we are not all that bad," Ethan mused.

"I get it Ethan," Max said, nodding. "Have you ever read a book or watched a movie where the gargoyles or witches are not attacking people or raising the dead?"

They sat down on the curb to continue their rant on how the quotidian's liked to scare themselves with vampires, witches, werewolves, zombies, ghouls, aliens, and insects. They continued to top each other's examples until Spartan started to growl. His growling got louder then he let out a protective bark.

"He hears or sees something not right," Max told Ethan worriedly. "Come on, we better get back to the house now."

"Follow me, Max." Ethan grabbed Max's hand, not giving him a choice. The house was a block away and there weren't many people on the streets.

Holding Spartan's leash tightly, Max followed Ethan across the park. Midway, Spartan stopped, raised his lip in a snarl and displayed his fangs to a cluster of azalea bushes.

"What is it, boy?" Max asked. "Ethan, I think Spartan sees someone in the bushes."

"Max, I don't know if it is a rabbit or a robber, but we should get back to the house now," Ethan stated.

"Do you feel anything odd?" Max asked.

"Not really odd, but my ears are ringing and it is hurting my head," Ethan replied.

Spartan was not convinced that whatever was in the bushes was not going to hurt them. Yanking the leash out of Max's hand, he laid his two front legs down on the ground and stretched out his body. Twisting his head from side to side while stretching his back legs out behind him, Spartan began to morph into a larger, stockier creature.

"Oh no!" Max cried. "Spartan, stop, stop!" Max yelled, looking around to see if anyone was watching.

"What's happening here Max? Something you guys forgot to tell me about Spartan?"

"I can tell you it is not a rabbit in the bushes," Max replied. "It has to be bad and it must want to hurt us, or Spartan wouldn't be changing like this!"

Spartan burrowed into the bushes, cracking

branches, barking and growling. Anyone still sleeping in the houses around the park surely was no longer. Purple azalea petals floated into the air as Spartan worked his way through twenty feet of underbrush. A shrill cry stopped Spartan's progress. The azalea bushes parted and a young girl appeared, tethered by her shirt hem held fast in Spartan's fangs.

"It's just a little girl, maybe my age," Max said, surprised. "Spartan let her go; she is just a little girl."

Spartan did not let go, snorting at Max's command.

"What is your name and why were you following us?" Ethan asked the girl.

She did not respond. Spartan grunted and growled again.

"We are kids too; we are not going to hurt you," Ethan added.

The young girl looked at Ethan and then at Max. Her eyes. Ethan recognized those eyes. Her eyes made him feel like he was looking back at himself.

She was examining them as much as they were examining her. Max was holding on to Ethan so tightly that his hand was going numb. Considering his options, he tried to stay calm. This little girl was capable of more than she seemed. The first thing he had to do was to get Max back home safely. If Spartan tore the girl to pieces in a public park there would be a lot of questions and he could be put down. Who would believe that she was a DM or mirror man?

Ethan wondered why a little girl was sent to follow them. She was pretty and petite and seemed harmless next to Max, Spartan and him. Then he considered meeting Camille, Gretchen or even his mom in an alley and quickly realized that he could be in trouble if he underestimated her.

Air talking! He realized he could air talk with Max as well as Spartan. Keeping his eyes fixed on the girl, he cleared his mind and told Spartan and Max to go home and tell Ms. Senona that he needed her help.

"Don't go straight home. We don't know if there are more with her or if she was doing some recon work," Ethan explained. "Spartan, take Max the back way. Go the way you sneak out when you smell that fried chicken down the street."

Spartan cocked an eyebrow as Ethan continued. "I am going to take her attention away from you both, then try and confuse her. Leave normally, as if nothing is going on. Are we all clear?"

"Spartan, please let the poor girl down now. I think she is scared," Ethan asked in a calm voice.

Hesitating for dramatic effect, Spartan placed the girl on the ground. With one paw still on her shoulder he returned to his natural shape. The girl did not move or show any sign of emotion. Lifeless, she continued holding Ethan's gaze with her deep hollow stare.

"Good boy Spartan," Ethan murmured. "My friend and his dog need to get home now. How about you and I sit down on a bench? We can talk, or just watch the squirrels play in the park."

Spartan padded past Max, who turned to follow him out of the park. The girl tilted her head slightly but made no other movement. Her eyes did not leave Ethan's as the others slipped away.

Ethan took a step towards her but she backed away. Slowly, Ethan extended his hand. Breaking her gaze, she reached her own hand toward his and grabbed it. Her hand lay cold and motionless in his grip. She took small stumbling steps as if waking from a long night's sleep. A couple walking their dog approached them and smiled. Their dog growled but did not bark.

"Good morning kids, isn't it a lovely morning?" the couple asked as they passed.

Ethan and the girl ignore them. However, Ethan noted that the girl seemed to be walking a little better after they passed.

"Let's sit on this bench. If you want, you can tell me your interest in us. That would be cool. If not, at least tell me your name," Ethan said cautiously.

An awkward silence fell. Ethan thought of something he read in one of his dad's magazines about the 'silent sale'. The first one to say something makes or breaks the deal. He waited.

After nearly ten minutes, the girl said, "Emily," watching a squirrel race up a tree.

"I'm sorry, what's that?" Ethan asked hastily.

"My name. It is Emily," she repeated.

She seemed more animated, and turned to face him on the bench.

"Hi, Emily. I guess you already know my name," Ethan greeted her.

"Yes. Ethan Terrance Atticus Juniuson," Emily replied.

Hiding his surprise, Ethan said, "You said

that all in one breath. I don't think I can even do that!"

"I surprised you don't have more names, considering how old your father's family is. I thought it was interesting that your father added 'on' to the end of Junius," Emily commented.

Ethan wondered himself, but not about the 'on' or how many names he had. He wondered how much she knew and how she had transformed from zombie to sassy in half an hour. Ethan wondered if Max and Spartan had made it home safely. He wondered if he was distracting her or if she was now distracting him.

The park was busier now, with people walking dogs, strolling babies, and jogging. Some kids were walking with their parents while playing their video games.

"Well, what is the rest of your name?" Ethan asked, hoping for more information.

"Emily, just Emily," she answered. "Mother doesn't think we need to have more names. It would be confusing. Aren't you confused, Ethan? Wouldn't you like to do whatever you want to do and not have to follow their stupid rules all the time? You have amazing gifts and you would really enjoy my friends and me. We do whatever we want whenever we want and can have anything we want," Emily added.

Her voice had a slight accent that Ethan recognized. His father's plant manager had a similar accent.

"There is a flip side to everything in life. The elders teach that life is made up of the yin and the yang, good with bad and not one without the other. They have to balance each other out," Ethan explained to Emily.

"Don't you want to be my friend? We can go get ice cream right now and no one will stop us. Not even the elders," Emily assured him.

Carefully, Ethan told her that he had just had breakfast and was not hungry. Actually, ice cream sounded good since he hadn't had anything to eat since a granola bar before leaving the house.

"We know that your kind have a very specific diet, but I thought all of you enjoyed ice cream. I know it is one of my favorites," Emily persisted.

"It will be lunch time soon," Ethan said as he consulted his watch. "My friend's mom would be upset if I didn't eat what she prepared for me."

"You're not a baby anymore, Ethan. If your father hadn't changed the rules you would be having your coming of age ceremony next year. Camille and Jeremy would already be doing adult tasks and you wouldn't have any friends, besides ghost girl and little Max. No matter how old or young you are I would still be your friend," Emily said intently as she looked Ethan in the eyes.

Her eyes were still empty, the pupils like blue colored glass that didn't really see you. It occurred to him that most people didn't really make eye contact anymore. It was hard for Ethan to hold her gaze, knowing bits and pieces of information about what these mirror men had been doing to kids' minds.

Emily was staring at him like she was trying to bore into his soul. He was reminded of when his parents knew he was up to something but he was trying to shield it. Every so often she would twitch, tilt her head or disappear behind her soulless eyes for a minute, like someone was talking to her or pointing something out.

"My friends and I are different than regular kids; we have a really special bond," Ethan insisted.

Emily smiled with her lips only. "I know

that you are different. We have been following your kind for a few years now. I really like having friends like you, with special gifts. I can have as many of the other kind as I want but they bore me quickly. Your kind is special. But most people will never accept vampires, witches, seers, shifters, gargoyles, jinn, angels and so on."

Emily reached down and held Ethan's hand. "You see, I am not going to judge you like others will. I am not scared of you. We are better than our parents and the other adults that don't have time for us. They are so busy trying to hold on to their youth and prove that they are successful. They don't even notice us until we do something that makes them look either bad or amazing. That, too, is the double-edged sword that gives us anything and everything that we want," Emily concluded.

Ethan found himself listening to her argument. Although it made a certain sense, he knew that he didn't agree with what she and her kind were doing. They seemed more like terrorists than freedom fighters, which was how he saw the Children of the Others.

"It is time for me to go, Ethan," she said abruptly, breaking her stare. "I am sorry that we didn't get to have that ice cream together. I know we will meet again. Think about what I told you."

Moving rapidly, she disappeared around the bushes where they had first found her. He wanted to follow her, but stopped himself. This was a recon mission, not a search and destroy mission, to use some video war game lingo.

"Ethan, my dear are you alright?" Senona hurried toward him.

"I am fine Madame," Ethan replied.

"Jeremy stayed with Max and Spartan. He wasn't too happy staying behind but he knows better than to argue with me," Senona assured him.

Ethan could only imagine the scene if Jeremy had come to the park and saw a mirror man sitting on the bench with him. A memory of their escape from the Asylum flashed to mind. His fury as they fought off hell hounds would be dwarfed by his anger towards a mirror man.

"Yeah that was probably a good idea," Ethan agreed.

"I am sorry that this happened to you today Ethan. Unfortunately, it had to happen sooner or later. As far as I am concerned, you handled everything better than most adults would have. I am most impressed with the way you were able to get Max and Spartan away safely without her suspecting anything."

"Did you know that something was wrong or did she sneak past your magical trappings?" Ethan asked.

"Be assured that the minute I felt Max's energy change I was working on my next move," Senona replied comfortingly.

"It was like she knew where we were going to be, but she had a hard time engaging us at first," Ethan thought out loud. "She didn't want to hurt us, but she did want something."

Senona pulled Ethan closer to her as they left the park. She used a bit of magic to calm his mind and called a shroud of natural chaos to shield them, just in case they were followed. Back in the house, Senona used the circle room to deliver the news to the community.

Ethan looked at Max and rubbed his head. "You were awesome out there today my little brother from another mother!"

"You, Spartan were BEAST," Ethan continued, "I mean like over the top. I never knew you had special gifts, too!" Spartan jumped into his lap and rolled over, licking Ethan's face and play growling.

"Jeremy you need to stay out of trouble, because it is not safe for Max to walk Spartan alone out there," Ethan added looking at his friend.

Blustering, Jeremy replied, "Now that you know how big and bad Spartan can be, I don't think any of us have to worry when he is with us."

"What if he wasn't with us? What if there were more than just one little girl? I think we need to get together in the Serenity Channel and make plans before there is a next time," Ethan responded.

"Mom says we are gathering tomorrow at the Row of Oaks, both children and elders, to discuss the mirror men threat. Well, mirror girl now, I guess," Jeremy told Ethan. "You are right though, I have been careless in my behavior lately. I am supposed to be teaching you survival skills. Thanks for securing my little brother and Spartan's safety at your own risk," Jeremy added humbly.

Ethan put him in a head lock and said, "Let's get those lines finished so we can play the rest of the day. Oh yeah, you also owe me an ice cream after lunch or I am going to go find Emily and take her up on her offer."

"ICE CREAM? Emily? What are you talking about?" Jeremy asked.

Racing him down the stairs, Ethan began his story.

CHAPTER FOUR

REALLY?

"I don't ever remember it being this hot so early in the spring," Jeremy complained. He licked his ice cream cone faster, hoping to not spill any more.

Max was having the same challenges as his big brother, who had convinced him that eating ice cream in a cone was the best way to enjoy it.

"I suggested that you eat it out of a cup like the rest of the kids," Luis observed, watching his boy struggle to finish his triple scoop ice cream cone.

"When I am big as you are, Dad, I will be able to finish a cone in two bites, eliminating the need to lick completely," Jeremy replied.

Reaching over to wipe ice cream from her husband's chin, Senona said, "I can't take any of my boys out in public without them making a mess."

"You know I do that just so you will have to clean me up, my love." Luis retorted, raising one eye brow and smiling at his wife.

"Really Dad, really Mom, TMI ! Do you have to even talk like that out in public? Dial it back," Jeremy asserted, looking at Max for agreement.

Jeremy was at the age where he had begun to find his parents somewhat embarrassing. He liked the idea that they were still in love but he felt uncomfortable with their blatant displays of affection. It was bad enough in the house, but in front of his friends or in public was intolerable.

"I think it is kind of cute," Gretchen blurted out, holding her hands up with her fingers in the shape of a heart framing Senona and Luis.

"Seeing older people who still love each other is great. People today think that everything disposable, including marriage and family," Mercy stated.

Senona looked at Luis, and then Mercy. "I am not sure about the 'old' part, but you are right, Mercy. Luis is still my shining knight, my hero!"

"My parents act the same way. I kind of agree with both of you, though. Having your parents flirt in front of you is weird, but it's cool that they still love each other so much," Ethan commented.

"That's why our families are such good friends. Each time your parents have moved nearby we see them still so happy together, just like Luis and me. Of course, when you have that kind of love, losing it as Gregory and Jonathan have can be heart breaking. It could take centuries to find a new mate," Senona replied.

"My father will never replace my mother because she is..." Camille stopped abruptly.

"It's alright," Mercy interrupted, "we have been talking a lot about family stuff lately. With Camille close to her coming of age, she has all sorts of new issues with her mind and body."

"Really Mercy? As if talking about true love wasn't enough, now you have to bring up my body and mind?" Camille snorted.

"Well, the body part is pretty obvious," Gretchen giggled, shrugging her shoulders.

Mercy and Senona smiled and laughed softly, covering it with a quick cough.

The boys, including Luis, knew better than to enter a discussion about the female body.

"So what if I am getting more curves to my body?" Camille asked sharply. Looking at Jeremy she added, "You started this, you know."

Turning to Ethan, Camille continued, "Why you don't have anything to add, being a male vampire?"

Confused, Ethan attempted to stare in her eyes and replied, "My father taught me one lesson about dealing with the opposite sex."

"Just one lesson, what's that?" Camille questioned.

Calmly, Ethan repeated, 'Never discuss a woman's hair style, weight, or figure, even if asked directly.' He says learning that a few hundred years earlier would have saved him a lot of difficulty."

Camille paused thoughtfully. "That is good advice; I suppose being that old has some benefits in relationships. Maybe some others should heed those words of wisdom," Camille suggested pointedly.

Jeremy laughed awkwardly, and then asked Ethan, "So what should I say if a woman asks one of those questions?"

"Change the subject to yourself, politics or

sports or shove food in your mouth so you can't say anything," Ethan informed him.

"Looks like I have one less lesson to teach Jeremy and Max," Luis sighed.

"Are we finished with ice cream? I think it is time to head back to the house. We wanted to ask if you would like to join us for a progressive summer vacation this year," Senona suggested.

"What is progressive summer vacation?" Gretchen looked excited.

"A progressive summer vacation involves visiting more than one destination and sharing responsibilities with other families," Senona explained. "We were thinking of travelling up the east coast, staying with friends, in hotels, or camping along the way. Some of us will have to work at certain times, but another adult will continue that segment of the trip."

"I think that would be awesome!" Ethan replied.

"That would a blast!" Jeremy added.

"If we make it to the state champions in soccer I won't be able to go," Camille said with disappointment.

"We already talked about that, my dear," Senona reassured her. "We have decided to wait until those games are over. Besides your schools get out three weeks earlier than the school in the northeast so it will work out perfectly."

"What troubling you?" Senona turned to Max, sensing her son was pondering something. "You are going to come with us too," she reassured him.

"No, I understand the progressive vacation trip, Mom," Max replied. "I was still trying to figure out what you were talking about when..."

Ethan interrupted. "Uh, it's alright Madame; I will talk with Max later about what's confusing him."

"So Max what is it you are confused about?" Senona persisted.

"When Mercy was talking about Camille's body and mind changes, did she mean her breasts getting larger?" Max replied.

Camille turned beet red with embarrassment while everyone else stifled laughs.

"Really?!" Camille huffed. "Yes, Max my breasts are changing." She glared at him, and then relented with a smile. Mercy she gave a gentle kick in the shin as they headed across the park.

CHAPTER FIVE

SURPRISE GUEST

"He's doing well," Senona told Helen, who called just after noon to check on Ethan.

"Aren't you the funny one?" she continued after a moment. "It isn't that I *can't* get up early; I just enjoy my beauty sleep." Senona ended the call after confirming their plans to meet that night at the Row of Oaks.

"... believe that the Trojans pulled the horse inside the castle to the altar and then just went to bed," Ethan exclaimed.

Camille, Gretchen, Jeremy and Max were hanging out in the family room, listening to Ethan retell the story of the Trojan horse.

"I don't even open a fruit bar without checking it out first," a voice commented from the doorway.

An uneasy silence fell over the room as they turned to look.

"What are you doing here?" Gretchen demanded.

"How did you get into my house?" Jeremy asked, startled.

Senona followed the guest into the room of questions. "I ran into him while I was out for my walk. We started to catch up. He told me that Ethan was in his class this year and they had become pretty good friends," she explained.

"So did you have to bring him home?" Jeremy asked, not even trying to hide his annoyance.

"Where are your manners, Jeremy? He will be attending tonight's council meeting representing his kind. I thought he could hang out with you guys for a few hours and then we could all go together," Jeremy's mother reasoned.

Ethan was confused by the irritation shown towards his friend from school. His hunch had been correct, after all – his friend was gifted, too, which made Jeremy's coolness even stranger.

"It's alright Madame, I will leave."

"You can stay," Camille offered reluctantly.

"Buenos!" Senona replied "Play nice and we will all be leaving in a few hours. Ethan, I spoke with your mother and they are going to meet us there," Senona added before leaving.

Thick silence blanketed the room. Ethan tried to decipher the uncomfortable emotions clouding the air. Gretchen and Jeremy were clearly angry. Camille seemed frustrated but intrigued. Max was sort of right there with Ethan because he didn't really know the guy.

"I didn't plan to come here and ruin your afternoon," he addressed the room.

"Gabriel, I didn't know that you were like us!" Ethan interrupted.

"He is not like us, not at all. Don't let him fool you Ethan," Gretchen blurted.

Becoming a little frustrated himself, Ethan asked, "So you have gifts, you don't have gifts, your parents have gifts? What is it?"

Gabriel surveyed everyone in the room. He knew each of them well, in some ways better than they knew themselves. Despite that, he could not control any of them unless they were interfering with his mission. He paused carefully before answering, briefly wondering why he had accepted Ms. Senona's invitation in the first place.

Gabriel's features were small but well defined. His shoulder length dark hair always seemed to feather back from his green eyes that were the talk of all the girls in school. The boys on the other hand thought he looked gay and weren't hesitant to say so behind his back. He blamed his tall, lean body on a fast metabolism, since he loved to finish his friends' lunches. He spoke clear precise English but on occasion would slip into French, Spanish, Mandarin or Portuguese. Purportedly, his family was military and he moved a lot.

Gabriel cleared his throat. "It is kind of complicated, but if you will let me explain..." "This ought to be good!" Gretchen snorted.

"Come on, you guys! Let me hear what Gabriel has to say. None of you have ever even mentioned him. You only introduced me because we bumped into him at the Black Eyed Peas concert in Atlanta," Ethan pointed out.

"Well, if I knew that the boy you were talking about was this Gabriel, I would have had a lot to say about him!" Gretchen replied.

Ethan stared at Gretchen, raising one eye

brow and telling her in whisper-speak to stop.

"Alright Gabriel, I obviously don't know you like they seem to know you. Why don't you explain it to me, your friend?" Ethan said as he pulled a chair over for Gabriel.

"To be fair to all of you, I have been less than honest in our past encounters. Gretchen, I am sorry for the way events developed when you were younger. I didn't have any control over the situation," Gabriel began.

Gretchen leaned her head back and a single tear rolled down her cheek.

"First, I would like to explain that I am always placed into a situation for the good of the person that has requested me. I do try very hard to be compassionate towards others affected by my actions, although they are not my first priority," Gabriel began. "I know that some of you have met me in different forms over the years and that too is something I cannot control."

"So what can you do if you don't control anything?" Camille asked from the arm of Gretchen's chair.

"Most of the time I am placed in a situation to observe closely or deliver a message. Very rarely do I ever have to interact directly if I am fulfilling my responsibilities," Gabriel clarified.

"Ok, so I get that you have some gifts, but what are you? I mean, I am of vampire lineage, Jeremy is witch and gargoyle, Camille is mystic and shifter, and Gretchen a ghoster. So what is your lineage?" Ethan persisted.

"He's an angel," Max declared. "I can see his aura around him. I have seen angels before," Max added.

Ethan stared at Max as if he had pop rocks for lunch. "An angel, Max? Really? You're kidding me, right?" Ethan looked at his friends who were curiously quiet.

"I mean it is not like I don't think that there are angels. But aren't they supposed to have wings, halos, and use a surreal loving voice when they speak?" Ethan chuckled.

"Not exactly what you were expecting then," Camille replied drily. "Yeah, Gabriel is a real angel."

"WOW, I feel just like I did that time in The Whispering V when you guys introduced me to ghosts. Or when I found out that I am a vampire and my best friends are witches, mystics and gargoyles. I am going to have to start checking out everyone more carefully;

next you will be telling me that zombies are real too," Ethan sighed.

"Zombies from the movies don't really exist, but they are pretty scary and make for good discussion," Gabriel assured him, amused.

"Angels never had wings," Gabriel continued. "That was a human creation to symbolize how we travel through time and space. Halos are just another symbol of our radiant energy, which allows us to break the time-space continuum. Some of us carry swords for smiting, but we would look kind of weird walking down the street in flowing robes. We don't sparkle and we don't only represent Christian faiths," Gabriel summarized.

"I guess I never really thought about angels other than those in Christmas stories and guardian angels," Ethan mused.

"That's like thinking all vampires suck blood through fangs and turn into bats, or that gargoyles turn into stone at dawn, or better yet, that witches all have warts, keep black cats and ride broom sticks. All of which you know is mostly false. Well, except the riding of broom sticks; I think a lot still use those. Angels are no different," Gabriel shrugged.

"There is nothing normal about you, Gabriel," Gretchen muttered.

"I know that the passing of your mother was hard, Gretchen. I was sent to comfort her through you, not to save her. I followed through on my responsibly and she moved on peacefully, and, if I can add, is doing quite well. I have been around for many millennia. If I were to regret all my questionable actions, nothing would get done," Gabriel explained.

Gabriel could feel Gretchen's pain like a sword through his heart, so he was careful in his next words.

"I do know that you are hurting, Gretchen and I am sorry. If there was any way that I could have saved your mother, I would have." Gabriel knew his words were only partially true and fortunately he wouldn't have to stand by them. "She was sick when I arrived and there was nothing that anyone could do at that point. Everyone in your community and the medical community had done all that they could to ease her pain and suffering as she was overcome by the cancer. I was asked only to comfort her and nurture you so she could have a few more months with you. She made the choice to die rather than..."

Camille interrupted Gabriel. "Look Gabriel,

we are not little kids anymore; we get it. I don't think we have to put Gretchen through all this again. So what is it this time? Are you here to keep a watchful eye over us until Ethan's coming of age? Do the elders feel that our generation lacks proper commitment to the tenets, so they sent you to baby-sit?"

She didn't expect a straight answer and therefore tried, albeit unsuccessfully, to read his thoughts.

"Why is everyone so concerned about what we are doing, anyway? Our parents are concerned, the elders are concerned and now the DM's are concerned. Are we that special? I sure don't feel like it." Jeremy vented his frustration by punching a harmless throw pillow.

"Me neither," Ethan agreed. "There are all types of predators in the world. They can't watch us every second and expect us to have a healthy childhood. They have to trust that we have learned the lessons that they have taught us."

"My brother said many years ago that 'even a hero is a social deviant'," Gabriel observed, seeing in their souls heroes and deviants like himself.

"Gabriel, if you have to be here will you

at least speak so we can understand what you are talking about?" Gretchen suggested, giving him a half-hearted smile.

"My mother told me that 'it is not difficult to deceive the first time, because the deceived possesses no antibodies, but be better prepared the next time, because there is always a next time'," Gretchen added. "I will try not to hate you with every ounce of my being, but I WILL be watching you."

"I can live with that," Gabriel replied.

"I guess you're the go-to guy in the realm of divinations and stuff?" Ethan changed the subject.

Gabriel responded cautiously. "Pretty much anything goes if I need it. But if I abuse it then I am punished. Like last year, when I started a fire under that boy's pants. You remember, the one that was picking on your dragon story. I thought it was very good, by the way."

"That *was* you! I thought maybe it was me and I had some ability that I haven't been able to use since then," Ethan laughed.

"I would have loved to have seen that," Jeremy exclaimed.

"Well, I had a lot of explaining to do for that stunt," Gabriel admitted. "It was funny though and the kid deserved it for any number of the stupid things he did daily."

"Did you know that I made this guy's voice change to a girl's after he said that my mother looked like a Spice girl?"Jeremy boasted.

The girls looked at each other and shook their heads at their childishness.

"We are going to see if we can help Ms. Senona with anything for tonight's gathering while you boys talk about your silly games, and who has the bigger set," Camille said. "Coming with us Max?"

Max shook his head and turned to the other boys who were laughing at something that Ethan had just said.

"Not you too Max," Camille groaned. "Come on, Gretchen. Let's get out of here before we have to shovel our way out."

CHAPTER SIX

ROW OF OAKS

Luis pulled carefully off the paved road, his van full of family and friends. Just moments earlier his passengers were singing and gossiping loudly. Now the silence of a cemetery crypt settled in van. Ethan, Max and Gretchen had never before attended an event on this historical property. Camille and Jeremy had been there once before, for protection. An attack on a group of witches at a festival caused many of the children to be brought there for safety.

"This brings back some eerie memories," Jeremy whispered.

Senona reached back and squeezed her son's hand for reassurance. For a change, he didn't pull away.

Jeremy remembered Nanna Chu's words that long ago day. 'You kids have nothing to worry about once we get through those gates,' the old crone had promised.

The plantation had been sacred land since the 1700's, when a good man named Noble Jones granted safe haven for the Others. In return, they provided sacred herbs, potions and assistance with a new type of construction he was trying.

Legend holds that Noble Jones still stands at the gates of his estate. He can be seen walking the Avenue of Oaks keeping watch over his friends and visitors.

As they approached the entrance, the huge ironwork gates broke open and slowly spread as far apart as they could. Jeremy stared at the gates as they entered, wanting to catch a glimpse of Noble Jones. No such luck this visit.

Once they had passed through the gates, plenty of activity became visible that was hidden from the road. Men and boys were directing vehicles to designated parking areas. Others stood in a circle to allow the materialization of guests from thin air. Helicopters could be heard coming and going in a distant part of the estate.

The children waited patiently as Luis maneuvered the custom Sprinter van into his delegated spot. Once parked, everyone gathered the personal items they needed for the council meeting. Camille took the longest as she had to fit everything into her saddle bag. Jeremy, Max, Ethan or Gretchen would not comment on the contents of her bag after last year's St. Patrick's Day events. That bag had been a life-saver, in more ways than one.

No sooner were they out of the van when some elves came up and handed them each a crystal. "Yours to keep close, yours to keep," one after the other repeated, as they moved methodically through the crowd.

"Black onyx, I *knew* that is what they were going to give us tonight," Jeremy commented as he carefully examined his stone.

"Why did you think it was going to be black onyx?" Ethan asked.

He pocketed it with his other stones and replied, "Its protection and energy shielding is good. But tonight it will be used for grounding and centering, which will allow the entire assembly to meditate together."

"That little stone can do all that? Cool!" Gretchen replied. "What are the other stones you have there for?"

"Bloodstone is my warrior stone, just in

case I have to garg out and help my dad. Tourmaline is to harmonize my left and right brain so I can be even stronger and better balanced," Jeremy explained.

"I hope that tourmaline is your largest stone, because harmonizing your brain could take a lot of energy," Camille quipped.

Jeremy pointedly ignored her and hurried to catch up to his parents. Senona was pleasantly surprised that Jeremy did not engage with Camille. His enjoyment at sharing his knowledge outweighed his need to banter.

"Alright everyone, remember where we parked, just in case we get separated later," Senona suggested.

The children were jostled as they moved through the growing crowd. Grey-robed men and woman lined the perimeter of the property, keeping a magical boundary. Thousands of people of all ages, races and sizes stretched as far as the eye could see, their varied garb a kaleidoscope of bright colors.

"Are they all like us?" Ethan asked Luis as he walked at a near trot.

"If you mean Others, then I suppose the

answer is no. Some are without gifts, but they work with us and don't fear us," Luis replied.

Ethan thought about that as they wove between clusters of conversing visitors. To be known as different, but have that not matter was a new concept. Actually, the non-gifted people were the different ones tonight, he realized.

Three young women with cat's eyes scurried around, asking for any electronic devices to be placed in bags which they would manage until after council meeting. "Please deposit all phones, tablets, cameras, games, watches, and hearing aids into the Bags of Trust," they repeated over and over as guests rummaged for electronic items.

"Why aren't they asking us? Why don't they stop everyone?" Gretchen asked.

"They are the Seekers," a melodic voice responded from behind them.

"Mom!" Ethan shouted. He turned around and hugged her quickly.

"I missed you so much," Helen told Ethan as she hugged him back.

"The Seekers are able to hone in on what is set into their conscious and subconscious minds," Helen continued. "They focus on nothing else but their mission."

"Crazy thing, though. They will not forget what they got from whom and at the end of the gathering they will return everything to the correct person without one mistake," Mercy added, impressed.

"So what's the big deal with the electronic devices?" Gretchen asked.

"First, it is rude to have phones and games being played and going off during assemblies. Second, I have a feeling it has something to do with the topic of the meeting," Mercy explained.

"Multimedia devices may be a distraction, but I couldn't live without my iPhone!" Camille replied.

"I know! I am sure you will be the first to have an implant or something when that technology is available," Mercy agreed, shaking her head.

"Who says that they don't already have that technology already?" Jeremy interrupted.

"A fellow conspiracy theorist," Mercy observed dryly.

"Pick up the pace, little ones," Luis shouted from ahead.

"It's hard to keep up with a man who has a stride three steps long," Camille complained cheerfully.

"It's alright to use magic here," Senona offered. She floated easily in her husband's draft.

"Cool," Max replied and followed his mom's lead. The old crone grinned at Max as he caught up with her.

"Look; there's Gabriel up there alongside my father," Ethan exclaimed. He pointed in the direction of a side porch of the plantation house.

"I thought that Gabriel was behind us this whole time," Jeremy commented. "Just goes to show you how sneaky he is."

"What is Gabriel doing with my father?" Ethan questioned.

His mother replied, "I am sure that the elders requested something from him."

A gong rang out over the assembly of Others. Everyone quickened their pace by whatever means possible to prepare for the opening of the council meeting.

Acres of Others flooded the live oak shrouded landscape. The variety of ages, sizes, nationalities and beliefs represented demonstrated a unity of purpose unseen in a millennium.

The younger attendees waited restlessly in the back of the gathering, watched over by a group of elves. They were too young take part in the formal opening ceremony, which included blessings, burning of incense that the children recognized as cedar and lots of chanting. They listened to the introduction of elders and global council representatives, some of whom performed ancient rituals and the sacred rites. The formalities took nearly an hour. A white noise spell seemed to linger for minutes at a time to prevent the children from hearing too much.

"I don't see why they wanted us to come if they weren't going to let us be part of the rituals," one young girl complained.

Camille raised an eyebrow, commenting, "It is an honor to be invited to this massive of a gathering before our coming of age."

This was Ethan's first time to any gathering this large. He paid very close attention to the rites, or at least as many as he could understand since many were recited in other languages. On occasion Ethan would tap Camille on the shoulder and ask her what the elders were saying. Camille was only too happy to show off how much she knew by giving Ethan a brief description.

The elves finally returned the children to their families, having to wake a few of the younger ones. Their family members brought the children in close to them, like birds tucking in young fledglings under their wings.

A tall man with slightly tanned skin approached the podium on the balcony.

"Welcome to all our children that are here to share in this assembly." He bellowed without the use of a microphone, yet could be heard as clearly as if he were speaking in a small room.

"Who is he?" Ethan asked Camille.

"That is Lord Bashshar. He exists between worlds and is one of the only elders that possess almost all of our gifts," Ethan's mom replied, sensing that Camille was not going to respond.

Camille released a little gasp. She had heard stories of Bashshar and was never sure if he was real or only an imaginary elder to keep everyone in check.

"So he is a sage as well?" Ethan asked.

He had just started to learn about the different hierarchies in the magical world and their associated levels of respect.

"Well, Lord Bashshar could very well be a sage since his family has been around for longer than anyone can remember. It is rumored that he is from the direct blood line of Odin. Lord Bashshar has chosen a path as a teacher, leader and counselor to our kind."

"We are here as many tribes of the enlightened ones," the voice resonated, "but we also share this night with a small ensemble of humans who have not yet realized their gifts. They are aware of the troubling times that we now endure. Do not fear them for they do not fear us. They wish only to bring down these predators that have created unrest and torment among our young ones. They too have lost young ones to the evil that preys upon innocent adolescents."

Lord Bashshar paused; he appeared to be communicating with others that were not present at the Row of Oaks. This allowed time for the crowd to rumble amongst themselves.

"What is he doing?" Gretchen asked.

Senona replied, "Lord Bashshar is communicating with many assemblies at one time. There are probably ten million or more that have gathered for this event around the world."

"Wow, ten million others around the world! That is a lot of us; now I am not so worried," Ethan exclaimed in relief.

Camille shook her head. "You guys are

not the smartest, are you? Ten million of us versus who knows how many of the DM's, and then add six billion nine hundred thousand quotidians. That means that we are outnumbered 7000 to 1, if the quotidians side with the DM's, which with those odds they probably would."

While the others were thinking about it, Ethan retorted, "I'll take those odds. We have amazing gifts and work together better than most people I know."

"That is the reason that I requested the children attend this evening," Lord Bashshar announced. He asked Ethan to repeat what he had just told his friends.

"Sir, My Lord, Mr. Bashshar, I said," Ethan paused, wondering how Lord Bashshar had heard his voice in the noise of the masses.

As Ethan spoke he felt himself being somehow raised into the air. "I said that even though there are few of us and many mirror men or DM's and humans, I feel that with our gifts and because my friends and I work so well together, I still like our odds." Ethan stopped and took a nervous breath, hoping that he had repeated himself clearly.

Once returned to the ground, Ethan

shuffled closer to his mother and friends, seeking safety in numbers.

"Our children are wise and have great strength in them. This child is the youngest of the vampires, son of Lord Atticus and born by a gift of selflessness with Mistress Helen. We must all have the same faith that someone so young and innocent has in our pursuit of this plague that has taken so many of our children," Lord Bashshar declared, pausing for a few moments as he gazed across the crowded landscape.

Jeremy took the opportunity to give Ethan a punch in the arm, saying, "Way to go vampboy, I guess all your training and teaching is paying off."

Ethan looked at Camille and Gretchen. They were not as impressed as Jeremy was with Lord Bashshar singling Ethan out.

Lord Bashshar continued, stating that he had already held counsel with the world elders and that a plan was being designed to battle these mirror men.

"Lord Atticus and a small regiment of others have followed this plague since the first attack two years ago at the Beltane festival. Atticus will now update all of us on what we are looking at from this threat."

CHAPTER SEVEN

PLAN OF ATTACK

A tticus stepped forward and cupped Lord Bashshar's hand, while lowering his head in a gesture of respect and loyalty.

Camille, Ethan, Jeremy, Max and Gretchen watched their formalities intently.

"Many greetings, my friends," Atticus began. "It has been a troubling two years for us and even more so for many others in our community. We have learned much but still not enough about this outbreak that is spreading throughout the world. We have learned that its main target is our youth, both other and human. We are still uncertain how this infection is initiated or whether it is even permanent. In the cases where we have captured a few of the carriers they have all deceased in short manner. There is no evidence of any foul play or mistreatment by the mirror men, as our children have nicknamed them."

"How is it that you and your warriors have not been able to discover the source? You say that our greatest seers, mystics and scribes have not been enlightened by the gods on this pestilence that feeds on the youth?" a representative shouted out.

"Might it be possible that an alien life form from another planet is testing the youth of different races for their strengths and weaknesses? They would surely see that our children are the best physically, mentally and emotionally," another representative declared.

The crowd grumbled. Ethan, Jeremy Camille and Gretchen looked at each other, wondering what Atticus' response would be. Even they hadn't considered that the mirror men could be alien life forms.

Senona, shaking her head, turned to Helen. "There is always one in the crowd. It is not like we don't have enough issues in our own galaxy without having to bring in another one too."

"Atticus was prepared for the question, thanks to Gregory. It is always easier to think that some alien life form would create more harm than we already do for ourselves. Sometimes I would like to actually see an alien, just to suggest that the creatures of this world were not solely to blame for all of its destruction, hatred and pain," Helen replied.

"My friends, I assure you that there is no species in this galaxy we call the Milky Way that doesn't bleed as do we. We are certain a group exists with a specific agenda regarding all of our children. Although the children of the Others may indeed have all of those qualities, they are still young and can be influenced. Empty promises have lured our kind and civilians both throughout time. The children are only vessels for this mirror men organization to fulfill their mission," Atticus explained.

"Why did the children call them mirror men, if they are only children?" another shouted from the crowd.

"As many know, we were attacked by a child at a Beltane festival. When the young man, a child really, attacked his eyes glazed over. Some unknown energy or force possessed him and he was lost to us. The children described his eyes as mirrors, holding unimaginable deeds in their depths but reflecting back only your image," Atticus clarified.

The crowd rumbled again as parents and children stared into each other's eyes uneasily.

"Why the young children? How can they help with a militant quest? They are nowhere near as strong or as gifted as us older ones." Ethan recognized his friend Tyson's voice.

"If you have a plan, my Lord, I will assist you in penetrating their forces. I am still young and can pretend I am even younger," Tyson offered.

"Your honor is duly noted, Tyson," Atticus replied. "Somehow, whether it is through magic, social media or an informant, we know that whatever the mirror men are using only works on the young. Every one that we have seen or captured is no older than fifteen; however we don't know what happens as they age. Clearly this will be a learning curve for us as well but for now they have not communicate with or through anyone older," Atticus replied.

The crowd rumbled again and many of the parents pulled their children closer.

"We have seen evil and chaos in many varieties over the centuries. We have successfully fought when we were attacked directly. We defend from destruction all living creatures on mother earth and still fight against the everyday cruelties of this modern world. Now the threat is to our children. The irony is that we must ask the assistance of those we protect or we will have nothing to fight for. If all children become controlled by these mirror men, our future will cease to exist," Atticus said gravely.

"I have requested the assistance of the angel legion, led by Gabriel. We are going to have to place our children in harm's way to draw out the mirror men. We don't know when or where they will infect the next child. We do know that Gabriel has organized the angel legion to watch over huge areas of time and countless numbers of children." Atticus paused as chants of outrage broke out in the crowd.

"This is unheard of, placing our children into a war that we don't understand. We don't even know who we are fighting or what they want. We should have our seers send them a message asking for their demands," a young woman argued angrily, shrouding her two children under her cloak.

Before Atticus had a chance to respond, Gabriel vaulted from the seat where he had been fidgeting during the speeches.

"Foolish girl," Gabriel exclaimed. "How about I take your two children right now and offer them first? At least you won't have a chance to screw them up like your parents did you, at least before they were slain for selling magic herbs and ancient secrets over the internet."

"You are all very concerned, as you should be," Gabriel continued more gently. "Unless you take these drastic measures that your elders have laid out, none of you will have any hope of protecting your children. I have listened to their plan of attack and feel that it is worthy of my kind. I have agreed to assist with it," Gabriel declared.

Secretly, Gabriel didn't think this situation really affected him. He couldn't really care less if these groups lost any of their children, as fast as they seemed to reproduce. However, he had established an interesting bond with Ethan and Gretchen. Many lifetimes had passed since he last felt so protective, irrespective of the cost. He was not going to reveal that as long as he was rewarded for his efforts.

"I feel it would be in your interest to consider the plan of attack that Lord Atticus and his warriors have devised. We will do our part to keep the casualties as low as possible," Gabriel added.

Murmurs and protests grew louder as the debate began.

Atticus stood before the anxiously stirring crowd, collecting his thoughts for a difficult explanation for the plan of attack.

Atticus had always been fairly confident speaking to large groups. He had been speaking to family, friends and business partners since he was not much older than Ethan. The elders had chosen Atticus as their spokesman many years ago. Oration seemed to come naturally to him. When he would step out in front of a crowd and explain, direct or instruct there was little or no discussion afterward.

Naturally wouldn't have been the word that Atticus would have chosen. He spent a considerable amount of time preparing his addresses, working through every possible question as to limit any discussion. Atticus had learned from a mistake he made many years ago. He had spoken emotionally for a cause but had not thought out all the details. As a result, a loved one of his had been harmed. Atticus believed he had not clearly presented the severity of the issue, so appropriate safety measures were not taken.

Since then, Atticus would not so much as give a blessing without first working out the details. Helen was often the first person that he would share his thoughts with. Only sacred text or private information from the elders did not pass her eyes. Helen was well-schooled, holding a number of degrees that she had acquired over the years. Her special abilities enable her to sense the concerns of the many and she knew how quickly an issue could become serious.

She also had an amazing vocabulary. She delighted in choosing words that were clever or particularly descriptive. She would read his declarations, making just enough changes to engage his audience and keep their attention. Atticus never questioned Helen's changes, as long as she explained the new words to him in advance.

"Gabriel may have been very direct. He is correct in stating that we have exhausted every other option. We have studied and evaluated every location that these mirror men have infected multiple children. We have also noted which children they have repeatedly tried to take, but were unsuccessful," Atticus began.

An eerie silence lingered as the parents waited to hear which children were to be used for the attack. Clutching their children's hands tighter and holding them close, no one uttered a word as they waited for Atticus to continue.

"We have already spoken with our friends in locations where these attacks have occurred. These families and others have agreed to assist in our efforts around the globe. While this decision did not come without a heavy heart, they understand humanity as we know it is now in danger.

"We need to take action immediately. Specific children have been chosen to make contact with the mirror men. They will lead them back to us for questioning, or follow them when possible to gather information on the source of the infection. The children that will be involved in this critical mission will be addressed by the council over the next month.

"As many of you know, this threat has hit close to me as well. My own son and other children of my local community have been approached. Although the attacks failed, they occurred while we were not even a stone's cast away.

"Let this be a warning to each of us that this threat is not shy. It moves boldly and seems to know our every movement. If there is anything that you feel is out of the ordinary with your child, contact us quickly." Atticus looked out over the crowd, catching Helen and Ethan's eyes. Helen nodded in his direction.

"Do not make any drastic changes to your routines. Become more aware of your surroundings and trust that we will triumph. "Now let us close this gathering with the beautiful enchantments of Loretta McFallen."

The elders had told Lord Atticus that there was to be NO discussion after the plan of attack was explained. Atticus knew nothing better than to have a magical voice close the gathering, while the others opened the portals to the real time of the surrounding world.

Camille stepped back from the crowd. Normally she would have offered counterpoint to the melody dancing through the tangled worries of the guests. But a chill crept along her spine as memories of that maypole dance flickered back to life.

The mesmerizing vocals somehow guided the participants back along the Row of Oaks, comforting their departure. Camille considered the words of Lord Bashar, Gabriel and Atticus. She idly took the cotton bag handed to her by the cat-eyed creature, suddenly unsure of her path.

CHAPTER EIGHT

INTERVENTION

Over the course of the next few weeks no one was willing to discuss what was in store for the young ones. The only truth that was known was that this issue with the DM's had escalated beyond what any of the seers, mystics, priests or politicians had ever expected. Now they were readying themselves to help the children on their mission to somehow infiltrate this sinister group.

Camille sent out a message to all the children of the Others that were participating to meet her on Friday evening in the Serenity Channel. Jeremy and Gretchen both tried to contact Camille to see if there was something that she wanted them to bring up in the discussion. They had arranged this in the past for these types of forums so she didn't seem too bossy or arrogant. Like the symbol language they had developed after the festival, the prepared comments conveyed information while shielding any one from scrutiny.

Ethan had felt Camille's energy after the assembly at the Row of Oaks and knew that she was preparing herself, mentally and physically, for this challenge. Jeremy had told Ethan how Camille scored 7 goals total and slide tackled pretty much anyone that got close to her team, taking 3 yellow cards in 2 games. Just more evidence that Camille was getting stronger and more prepared for their mission.

Ethan had his own challenges. His father had started training him to control his vampire energy, something that he would normally not be taught until his coming of age. He was also being instructed on how to blend.

"It's like being invisible but without the magic or ghosting," his mother had explained.

He was capable of neither, he had admitted to Gretchen the previous week.

Friday arrived and everyone was pretty excited, not as much about the called meeting but because final exams were over. Only one week of school remained before summer vacation. The summer promised to be epic, with their travels up the southeastern coast to try to discover more about the DM's. Jeremy and Ethan had been calling each other nearly every night to talk about all the fun things they were planning. White water rafting, riding a 200 foot zip line, mud bogging on ATV's in the mountains, playing hide and seek in caves, sliding down monster water slides and camp fires every night with s'mores and, of course, ghost stories.

As eight o'clock approached, her father and Mercy asked Camille to sit with them in the study for a few minutes. Camille agreed, frustrated. She knew it was better to listen, else they would delay her time in the Serenity Channel. She entered to find Mercy, her father and Lilith waiting on her.

"I wasn't expecting to be confronted by everyone that lives in the house!" Camille exclaimed. "Can you just get to the point of this family meeting because I have something I have to do," Camille added tensely.

"Heading into the Serenity Channel. I know," Gregory replied.

Looking at him, she blurted angrily, "I

thought we promised not to read each other or snoop."

"That is no way to speak to our father, or me for that matter!" Mercy snapped. "Everyone knows about your meeting in the Serenity Channel tonight. Parents have been talking about it all week. *We* have been dealing with that so you could finish your exams without interruptions. Now that exams are over, we all need to talk," Mercy stated.

"You are not my mother and have no right telling me what I can or can't do. I have to go; I can't deal with this right now. Some of us are being used to lure in a serious threat this summer and we have to have a meeting about trust and sacrifice." Camille turned towards the door, which slammed shut as she approached it.

"Are you kidding me? You are going to lock me in the room so that I am late for a meeting that I called," Camille protested, glaring at her father, sister and cat.

"You are the one wasting time here," Mercy replied.

Camille rolled her eyes and snorted.

Calmly Gregory spoke. "Camille it is only 7:15pm, which gives you some time before your 8:00 pm meeting. If you two would both sit down and stop this childish bickering, we can address the concern at hand in a timely fashion."

"You are not going to stop me from addressing the others?" Camille asked her father uncertainly.

"Of course not, my dear. The other children need to know that you are working on some options concerning this serious issue. Mercy and I have talked about it at great length; we feel that after your experience in The Time Chamber Asylum you have much to offer these young ones. They all trust you and admire your commitment to our kind, whether they agree with you or not," Gregory explained.

"So then what is this powwow about?" Camille asked.

Gregory chuckled as he reminded himself that he was dealing with a teenage girl and not just his gifted seer, mystic, shape-shifting daughter. He had been through much in his life but his daughters' teen years always added a few more grey hairs.

"Camille, it's the way you are dealing with this that has lead me to having this 'powwow'," Gregory started but was interrupted by Mercy.

"It's the way you are dealing with a lot of things that has us worried. The way you attacked other players on the soccer field, the way you talk back to our father and the fact that you have been ignoring everyone that is trying to assist you, including Lilith," Mercy pointed out bluntly. Lilith, who had been sitting like a porcelain sculpture, rolled her head and purred.

Camille didn't say a word; she knew they were right.

Gregory continued, "My dear Camille, it is hard being a father to such an amazing young woman. An amazing young woman with many special gifts and responsibilities. I am your father and it is my responsibility to ensure that you manage those gifts and responsibilities properly. Soon you will be out on your own like Mercy and you will have to make your own choices and live with the results.

"I called this intervention because you need to focus your energy on being an amazing young woman, not just on the DM's or on soccer or school, or your gifts. If you focus on being that amazing young woman, you will be amazing in all those areas without having to work as hard on any one of them."

Camille started to cry; Mercy put her arm around her little sister. Gregory reached up from his chair and pulled both his daughters into his lap for a family embrace.

"I am sorry, Daddy; I just wanted to show you and the others that you have nothing to be concerned about. I can handle everything," Camille explained between sniffles.

Gregory sighed. "I was not there for your sister as much as I needed to be, but I have been here for you. There is nothing that you have to prove to me or anyone else. I am blessed to have the extra years in my life to share with you and your sister. You are both all the good parts of your mother's and my love for each other."

Mercy blushed slightly and rolled her eyes. "OK, Dad, we get it."

"I know that you don't want to be late for your meeting. Remember not to dictate to the other children. They don't all have the same passion as you, but they do understand the urgency of this issue. They will listen to you more if you are compassionate when giving them the details of the plan," Gregory suggested gently as he wiped the tears from Camille's face with cuff of his sleeve.

"I'm sorry Daddy; I will get a tissue," Camille

said, seeing her father clean her tears with his shirt.

"No, my dear, it is alright. I want you to get ready for your meeting and think about what we discussed," Gregory replied.

Camille started to stand when Lilith jumped into her lap, kneading and purring. Camille, Mercy and Gregory laughed. Lilith would not be left out of their family moment.

"Yes, I love you too. I will work on my attitude, starting tonight," Camille promised.

The door flung open as Camille went to leave. Six busy little fairies and brownies had been hovering outside, listening to the intervention.

"Alright you bunch, the excitement is over. Let Camille get to her meeting with the others," Gregory chastised the little winged creatures. They bumped and tumbled over each other, hurrying to follow Camille down the hall.

CHAPTER NINE

SAVING THE WORLD

C amille entered the Hive, drying off and silently preparing to enter the Serenity Channel. She left the usual offerings for her little friends that watched over her special place in her absence. After a few sips of water, she sat, crossed her legs and began the meditative process of entering the Serenity Channel.

She arrived to the welcome of her friends. They had arrived early, cautious not to upset Camille with tardiness. Camille was pleased to see that so many had come to listen and discuss the issue of the mirror men. The children covered the open meadow and clustered in the trees ringing the meeting space.

"I don't think I have ever seen so many kids

here at one time before," Camille murmured to Gretchen, who had appeared next to her.

"We are all worried about the severity of this issue and know that you have probably thought it through a million different ways. Take this as a compliment; we have faith in your planning," Gretchen replied.

"Well, some of them are also scared of you!" Ethan added from behind her.

"Yeah, about the way I have been acting lately ...."

"No words needed. Understood," Ethan interrupted.

"Well, you can say it to me!" Jeremy yelled. He jumped down from a nearby tree.

"Why were you up there?" Camille asked.

"I was waiting to see what kind of mood you were in. You screamed at me the other day for saving you a seat in the lunch room," Jeremy replied.

"Sorry about that Jeremy. I was having a bad day and thought you were just being nice because you wanted something." Camille sighed.

"Whatever." Jeremy shrugged. "So what have you seen and what do we have to do? I am ready to kick some DM's butt and find the bad guy behind this crazy stuff and take care of them, too. Then we can have the rest of the summer to mess around and relax!" Jeremy punctuated his enthusiasm for combat with some kind of karate/MMA moves.

"I wanted everyone together so that everyone understands both the plan and the danger," Camille clarified. She had learned from her father to give information and instruction once to prevent misunderstandings and confusion.

Jeremy whispered something to his tree and within minutes all the children gathered around Camille. She stepped onto a large root and was raised into the air to be seen and heard by all. Murmurings quieted and Camille closed her eyes, bowed her head and brought her hands together in thanksgiving.

She lowered her hands and opened her eyes, silencing even the trees.

"Thank you all for attending this meeting tonight. I wish we were here for fun and dreamscape rather than what we have to discuss. I have spent the last few weeks engaged in every form of mysticism and quantum connection I know. I have listened to seers, mystics and priests as they spoke with the elders. This poison has infected not only our kind, but the commoner as well. I assure you that using us as bait is the last resort to lure in these beasts." Camille paused and surveyed the reactions.

One young boy, not much older than nine, raised his hand as if he were in school. Gretchen giggled when Camille told him that he didn't have to raise his hand to speak.

"Well I was kind of wondering, what if one of these mirror men kids attacks us while we are in our house and no one can hear our cries for help? Or do we need to invite them in like vampires? No offense, Ethan," he added.

Snickers floated from the crowd.

"If they come into my house to attack me or my family I will tear them to pieces," one of the older shape shifters declared.

"Well if they try to get into our house I will rearrange every molecule in their body so they won't know what they are," another shouted.

Jeremy clapped his hands three times, leaving a ringing in everyone's ears for a few minutes.

"I agree that it would be tempting to tear up a little mirror men butt; however, let's allow Camille to answer Christopher's question properly before we all are turned into mirror men," Jeremy suggested when the ringing faded.

"Thank you Jeremy." Camille looked around the group. "Christopher has a valid question. The mirror men will not ask to be invited in. They will have you bring them into your home and then proceed to set up virtual lines of defense and offense. Remember, vampires can also enter your home without your invitation; however, it places an almost unbearable amount of stress on their bodies. Perhaps some of you would benefit from studying our own kind, rather than relying on information from internet searches and television characters. As the mirror men demonstrate, not all is as it is presented," Camille replied.

"I heard that the DM's need energy to power them up?" Gretchen asked to redirect Camille's attention.

"That is true," Camille replied. "We have learned that they seem to become very lethargic and disorientated when they have little energy. Ethan and Max experienced this a few weeks ago when one approached them early one morning. The DM's appear to be more active during the day, implying that the energy they need is similar to solar, kinetic or random energy. Their batteries, so to speak, seem to need regular recharging," Camille explained.

"They seem to infect only children; no adult has been to known to be affected. Our energy particularly attracts them, which is why we are being asked to go into the world and lure them out. Once they have been identified, our elders will handle things from there."

Some children began whispering and chattering about robots and cyborgs. "Many of us here have had minor encounters with the mirror men already. I assure you they are not robots; they are very human, at least on the outside," Ethan explained.

"They seem to know exactly what they want, but they do appear to communicate with someone or something. If asked a question unrelated to their agenda, they will take an extended time to answer," Camille continued.

"How will we notice that?" someone asked.

"Most kids are visceral, you know, instinctual in their responses rather than intuitive," Camille explained.

Most nodded, despite the truth that many

of them were more intuitive and perceptive than those 10 times their age.

Camille finished by reminding them to be aware of those around them. If they felt that a certain area contained a mirror man, they should mark it with the COTO sig for all to be aware.

"Does anyone have additional questions?" she added.

A tiny girl piped up. "The human children, how can we trust that they will not sacrifice us for their own safety?"

Camille replied, "The same way that they have to trust that we will not sacrifice them for ours."

The girl shook her head, unconvinced.

"The elders have put into place many safeguards and will never be far," Camille added, stepping down from the tree root.

As sounds of excited conversation began, Camille slipped into the trees for a moment of peace. The past year had been extremely stressful, with seeing her mother and Mercy coming home. Her coming of age ceremony was approaching. Her friends knew that even Camille needed help to get through tough issues, just like on St. Patrick's Day last year.

"Hey, wait up." Gretchen popped in view beside her.

"Don't think that you are going to get off that easy with us," Jeremy said, falling in behind her.

"You may not want to tell the others everything, but we deserve to know," Ethan insisted.

Camille stood silently, staring into the trees. She knew more than she was saying, and she also knew that secrets couldn't be kept from her friends.

"Sometimes I wonder what it would be like to be like them," she said softly, referring to the ordinary children. "They haven't got a clue about what is really going on around them. Their biggest concerns are if some boy likes them or if they beat some video game or how many social media friends they have and what they are saying. Not to mention their REALLY ridiculous concerns like who won some reality show that is more staged than a movie."

"Nice to see the real Camille back!" Jeremy laughed.

"My father thinks that I have been a little harsh lately. He is right. I have been hard on my real friends and I am sorry for that. Don't get me wrong, I like the gifts that I have. But there are sometimes I think that not knowing may be as magical as knowing all the time," Camille smiled ruefully.

No one responded at first, unsure how seriously to take Camille's confession. She was their unofficial leader, with high expectations they all strived to meet.

Finally, Ethan ventured, "I am still sort of new at all this stuff, but I think we are sort of like super heroes in a certain way.

"Seriously, think about it for a minute. Super heroes hide in the shadows, live dual lives and have to follow rules whether they like it or not. I am not delusional, I know that we are not comic book super heroes, but you know what I mean?" Ethan looked intently at his friends, anxious for their responses.

"As long as I can be Iron Man!" Jeremy decided.

"More like the Hulk!" Camille laughed, as Jeremy jumped on Ethan's back yelling "Hulk Smash!"

Camille's mood seemed to lift and she whispered with Gretchen as the boys ran around pretending to be super heroes. A few of the other children had followed them into the forest, eager to hear more about the mirror men, or just drawn into play by the noise of the boys.

"I do sometimes wish that I didn't have to think about everything that is constantly going on in the world," Camille confessed. "The boys seem to be carefree, no matter what is going on."

"It's a good thing that they come through for us when we need strength and stamina!" Zoe bounded up, followed by her identical twin sister Chloe. They were part Xanas, which basically meant they weren't the girls to bring home to mother. Only their hairstyles differentiated them. Zoe's hair hung dark and shiny down her back, while Chloe wore hers shoulder-length with bangs.

"Let's face it girls, we need those boys whether they are silly, dumb, funny ..."Chloe chanted, letting Zoe finish with... "or hot, sexy, and rich!"

"Us girls can handle most of what's going on, but it is still nice to know that there are guys out that will fight for us and carry us over a river if need be," Gretchen agreed.

"Exactly! Zoe, you always have to make everything about sex and you are only fifteen and haven't even had it yet," Chloe griped.

Zoe rolled her eyes. "Yeah, whatever. Like

you weren't thinking the same thing." Being identical twins and Xanas also, they knew everything about each other. Their coming of age ritual would be cancelled if they had sex with a boy or girl before the elders decided they were ready.

Camille changed the subject to avoid the Zoe/Chloe sister drama, thick with adolescent sexual frustration.

"You are all correct. No matter how much I try to not think about what is happening, it is still going to happen. However, I would love to be Catwoman, even though I am more like a mutant Emma Frost," Camille sighed dramatically.

"I want to be Red Sonja. She is sexy, smart and deadly!" Chloe declared.

"I guess I would be Bat Woman, or maybe Storm," Gretchen mused.

"Then that leaves me as the Scarlet Witch! It depends on my mood if I want to be good or bad, cause you know sometimes it is good to be bad" Zoe teased.

"So then why are super heroes not considered freaks, but we are?" Camille wondered.

"It's because the super hero's powers are created by random events, but our gifts can't be explained by a chemical spill or mutant bug bite," Chloe shrugged. "We are just ourselves."

"'Baby you were born this way...'" wailed Jeremy from a nearby tree.

"What you do is pretty amazing," Zoe chimed in. "You and the others will do whatever it takes to solve this mystery of the mirror men and life will get back to our kind of normal someday.

"But if you wore a sexy costume while you did it you may not be looked at as strangely," Zoe added naughtily.

Camille laughed, then jumped into the nearest tree whispering, "Meow, prrrr... I think I see some evil boys that we should capture for the authorities."

CHAPTER TEN

LET THE TRIP BEGIN

School was finished for the year and everyone had been promoted to the next grade. Camille's school had two soccer games left in the regional play-offs after winning the first round. The children were preparing themselves for a summer of adventure, while their parents were still arranging their work and vacation schedules. None of these concerns were nearly as important as the plan that the elders had set in motion to smoke out the mirror men and their master with the children's help.

"Ethan, what have you packed for the summer road trip?" Camille asked.

Ethan had spent a few hours with Camille's father learning how to read body language. He didn't understand how learning why people sit a certain way or look in a certain direction or how long it took them to answer a question was going to help him when he could just read their minds. Gregory assured him that these were significant observational skills that he needed to master. Ethan was glad Gregory couldn't read his mind on the subject.

"I haven't really packed much because I keep a lot of the stuff in the R.V. already," Ethan replied.

"That's right, your family likes this camping thing," Camille retorted. "Some would say that camping in a motor coach is not really camping."

"My mom feels that family time with limited interruptions from business or the internet is a good thing. Since my parents need a little more privacy than others, our motor coach is a perfect mesh of both worlds," Ethan explained defensively.

"You might find that you enjoy our type of camping," he continued, a little irritated. "You can only bring 3 bags of clothes and extras but that is not going to be a problem for you, knowing the way you can fill a bag." Ethan knew that Camille liked her luxuries but he also knew that she had been talking about the trip every day for the past month.

Camille smiled, acknowledging his joke. She wouldn't be roughing it too much by caravanning up the east coast in three motor coaches with eight families travelling with them off and on. She would have liked to use magic to travel a little faster, but she understood that they were on a mission as a community.

"I suppose I will be able to endure the road trip, as long as you boys don't start with your dumb jokes and burping contests," Camille said.

"What are you talking about? You and Gretchen beat us both at the burping competition last time. Jeremy won the gas attack!" Ethan replied indignantly.

Camille had tried to forget about the gas attack. "That boy eats way too many beans," she decided.

"You still have two soccer games left. Do you know yet where you are meeting up with us?" Ethan asked.

"More than likely it will be in North Carolina. That part of the trip will be grand because I will be travelling on my father's friend's G-6," Camille bragged.

"That sounds pretty cool. I have only been on an airplane twice and both times it was night. I don't remember much because I slept most of the time. My parents prefer to travel by land or water; I think flying in a private plane would be pretty beast though," Ethan said.

He went on to explain that he liked the R.V. the most because he had all his stuff with him and that they could make meals, sleep, use the bathroom and play games while his dad or Madera drove.

"Besides there is no way that one of the mirror men are going to get on our coach," Ethan added.

"That's a good point Ethan," Camille agreed. "That is probably why the elders decided to travel this way and camp so that we wouldn't attract any additional attention."

Realizing this made her more comfortable with the idea of camping.

"I have a feeling that someone just had an epiphany!" a voice commented from behind them.

Gabriel was standing only ten feet away and had been listening to their entire conversation.

"Really Gabriel, what is up with you dropping in whenever you feel like it, without even asking for permission?" Camille protested.

"And you wonder why certain people have problems with you."

Gabriel shrugged his shoulders and continued, "It amazes me you are so intelligent and gifted but the simple things are always so difficult for you to figure out, Camille."

Camille stared at Gabriel, not sure if she should take his comment as a compliment or an insult.

"I am sure that you will not be sharing in the experience of convoying or camping with us," Camille stated.

"As a matter of fact, I will be travelling part of the time with everyone," Gabriel replied.

"So travelling by motor coaches and camping was strategically planned by you and the elders for the purpose of controlling contact situations with the mirror men?" Camille asked.

"No need for me to say any more than you already know," Gabriel decided. "Please keep this information to yourselves. You should first think of the great experiences that you are all going to have. I remember hundreds of years ago the fun and work of travelling, the fond memories of friends and experiences we shared together."

Ethan was quite interested but Camille

wasn't up to listening to Gabriel reminisce about his travels.

"Besides you will be meeting and staying with others just like you along the way. It is the perfect opportunity for you and the others to get to know each other better as well as perfect some of your gifts. I would think that with your coming of age ceremony not that far off in the future that you, Camille, would cherish this time to grow," Gabriel said.

Bewildered, Camille looked at Ethan who was now sitting with his feet in the pool. "I suppose that this summer could be a good experience after all. I mean, if they had explained this earlier then I could have prepared better."

"I suppose it is better that we don't know anything more than we need to. This way we can keep it as real as possible. Right, Gabriel?" Ethan looked behind Camille where Gabriel was standing just moments ago, but no one was there.

"See, this is what frustrates me about him," Camille grumbled. "One minute he is here and the next he is gone. And I still had questions for him."

Shyly, Ethan lowered his head and reached

for Camille's hand. "I promise I will never do that to you."

Late Thursday evening three cars rolled into Ethan's driveway. Ethan had been standing like a foot soldier waiting for the others to arrive. Finally they were here, Ethan thought. His mother replied, "Patience, son. You know that they had to pack up their cars after work before coming here."

Helen walked out the front door towards Ethan who was making his way towards Jeremy and Max's van. Atticus had prepared the motor coach earlier in the day so when people arrived they could load their bags into the under coach compartments in an orderly fashion.

Max ran up to Ethan. "I am so excited about spending the whole summer with you."

Ethan agreed that it was going to be a fun and exciting trip.

"Hey Ethan what have you been up too?" a familiar voice rang out. Tyson, the older vampire boy he had met at the Beltane festival two years ago, jumped out of the van.

"I didn't know that you were coming with us!" Ethan exclaimed as he gave him a fist pump, hand smack, chest bump.

"Yeah, me neither. This is my step brother Chase, who is now living with us. His folks were lost in some astral plane thing they were doing. He is the same age as you and Jeremy. Anyway, he doesn't know anyone around here and the elders think that the DM's may have had something to do with my Uncle and Auntie's disappearance. So I was asked to roll with him and you guys," Tyson explained. "Not a bad gig if you can get it."

"That's cool," Jeremy said as he approached Tyson and Chase. "I'm Jeremy and this is my little brother Max." Jeremy put his hand out to fist bump Chase.

Chase stood for a moment and looked at Tyson. Tyson nodded his head in approval, so Chase fist bumped Jeremy and let Max give him an awkward hug.

"Sorry to hear about your mom and dad," Max said. "We are all friends here and we will help you with anything, well unless there's a dead body. Then I have to ask my parents what to do," Max added.

Chase looked curiously at Max.

"We all have our rules, and in our house if there is a dead body we are suppose to tell our parents," Jeremy rushed to explain. "Not that we have had any yet, but Max abides by all the rules and that is one of them."

"We have rules in our house, too," Tyson said. "We have to keep a log of all the bodies that we bury and where we buried them."

Jeremy, Ethan, Max and even Chase looked at him wide-eyed.

"Just messing with you guys," Tyson laughed. "Man you are easy!" Tyson walked off to greet the others.

"Looks like you boys just got punked. That's how they say it, right?" Senona said as she moved the boys into the motor coach.

Atticus and Luis stepped into the motor coach as everyone was settling down. The coach rocked a little as Luis entered, reminding Atticus that he needed to make some adjustments for the weight of nine passengers.

"Everyone ready on the inside?" Atticus asked of his passengers. He and Luis had already secured the basement doors and the tow vehicle for the six hour drive.

Helen affirmed and with that Atticus released the air brakes. They made a loud hissing sound as the bio diesel engine started to propel the vehicle forward. Deep under the sound of the coach, the sound of a cat purring reached Atticus' ear. He hit the brakes and engaged the air brakes, causing the motor coach to come to a stop before even making it out of the driveway.

"We have a stowaway!" Atticus announced.

Helen and Ethan recognized the purring and located its source as one of the bunks.

"I'll take care of this, my dear," Helen replied as she walked back, reached into the top bunk and pulled Daisy out from under a pillow.

"I have already explained that you were not allowed to come on this trip. We have your favorite pet sitter coming to spoil you," Helen explained to Daisy.

Daisy ignored everyone in the coach as Helen walked her to the front. Atticus shook his head as Daisy gave him a look of 'I almost got away with it.' Helen quickly returned to the coach after returning Daisy to the house. Helen smiled tightly at her husband, but with Atticus still shaking his head, she didn't say a word.

Once again the air brakes hissed and the coach moved out on to the road, roaring as it picked up speed. Everyone stayed seated and silent as they took in the passing lights of the city.

"Now that we are on the road, I will give you the plan for the next month," Senona announced. "We are going to be driving to North Carolina tonight, where we will meet up with the other coach. Once we have rendezvoused we are going to travel together to one of our Clann's property that I am sure you will all enjoy. They have horses and streams and near 30,000 acres of land to play on."

The boys began discussing all the things that they could do on that much land and how much fun they were going to have.

Senona, relieved that she had lost their attention for the time, sat down with Helen who was across from Chase.

"Chase, my name is Senona. I am Jeremy and Max's mother. Their father is Luis, up front there with Atticus, who is my best friend Helen's husband and Ethan's father." Senona smiled at him. "We are extremely sorry for all that you have gone through but we are very excited that you and Tyson are sharing this adventure with our boys."

Chase was silent for a few minutes as he had moved his eyes up to the front of the coach where Luis and Atticus were sitting. Returning his gaze to Senona, Chase queried, "Is it true that Mr. Luis is a 15 foot tall gargoyle who can tear a person apart with his pinky and that Mr. Atticus is one of the oldest vampires and he can drain all the blood from his victims in one bite?"

Silence fell over the motor coach, the only sound of the road rumbling beneath them.

"Chase what are thinking, or are you not thinking, with a question like that?!" Tyson yelped. "I am sorry you all for my little step bro's lack of manners."

Senona smiled at them both; it was not the first time that she had heard these stories told about her husband or Atticus. As a journalist she knew how to put a spin on everything.

"You are partially correct, Chase," Senona answered politely. "The truth is that Mr. Luis is one of the largest green builders in the southeast and after he reads the stories about himself he thinks that he is 50 feet tall and bullet proof. As far as tearing anything apart with his pinky, let's just say we will leave that in the bedroom where it belongs. "Now Mr. Atticus. Well, he has been known to drink a 64 ounce coffee without taking a breath. I have seen him drink two in a row before; no wonder he doesn't sleep well. Since there is 5 liters or 169 ounces of blood in the human body that would be pretty impressive even for someone as amazing as Atticus," Senona said with a smirk. "Don't believe everything you hear, Chase. If you do, well then I can make Luis cry like a baby and I have seen Atticus at a loss for words!"

Laughter filled the coach and even Chase forgot his fears in Senona's spell. He asked Ethan where the bathroom was, a sign that he was warming up to everyone.

"Why don't you give Chase and Tyson a tour of our crib on wheels?" Helen told Ethan.

"Mom, really, our crib on wheels? You're too old to call it a crib," Ethan replied.

As they started the nickel tour, Senona observed, "Why do the guys have all these stories told about them when us woman are pretty dangerous and amazing too?"

Helen replied, "I am just fine with the guys having to burden those tales. They know that the goddess will always be more powerful than them."

Ignoring the bait, the men returned to their conversation about work and alternative energy. Atticus was explaining how he was experimenting with some new solar technology that will help power the motor coach. Luis shared information about a new double wall insulation that maintained better temperature control. The boys huddled in the back of the coach.

"Let's pull an all-nighter and listen to music while we figure out what we are going to do for fun and how we are going to deal with these punk DM's," Jeremy said. "I bet the girls are already asleep!"

CHAPTER ELEVEN

NORTH CAROLINA

The girls' coach rolled over the North Carolina state line six hours after leaving Georgia with Gretchen, Chloe, Zoe, Mercy and Jia. Jia was an eastern elder's granddaughter who was attending school in America. She hoped to someday blend eastern and western philosophies in business and magic practices.

Chloe and Zoe's mother Monique had already explained the adventure. The girls were excited to be away from home and really didn't care much about the plan; as a matter of fact, they were not interested in sleep either. They had been listening and singing along to music from Katy Perry, Lady Gaga, Rhianna, Justin Bieber, Jesse J and other pop artists while Chloe and Zoe brushed Gretchen and Jia's hair.

"It is nice not having the boys around. They always make stupid comments when we brush each other's hair or go to the restroom together or sing along to music," Gretchen commented.

"That is unless we are singing some song by Eminem or Luke Bryan!" Chloe added.

They also listened to some of the stories Mercy shared with them of her adventures good and bad when she ran away after graduation.

"I can't believe you were living on the streets in Paris and Prague while modeling for magazines," Chloe exclaimed.

"Not some of my proudest moments," Mercy told them. "It was good that I could transform into a cat form, which helped with receiving generous food from bakeries."

"Where do you store your clothes, phone, money and I.D. when you shift?" Gretchen asked.

"Everyone is different," Mercy explained. "These are some of the things that you will learn after your coming of age. I suppose that it wouldn't be a secret to tell you mine though. I use a 5 gallon plastic gas can that I cut part of the top open and then tied a rope around it. No one ever picks up a nasty gas can with a rope tied around it," Mercy explained.

The girls looked at each other, thought about it and didn't ask any more questions on that topic.

"I think meeting Johnny Depp in person must have been awesome! You were in this form and not cat form when you met him?" Zoe asked. "Is he really as amazing as he seems in the movies?"

"Yes, I was in this form but the cat form may have worked too. To answer the second part of your question, he is even more awesome. He was not really acting when I met him in a Paris Café, he hadn't shaved in a few days and the shirt he was wearing was torn in three places," Mercy added.

"Did you get his autograph or something?" Zoe asked.

"No, that would have been very impolite. I did take a picture with my phone of him standing beside me," Mercy replied.

"No way, how did you do that?" Chloe asked out of sheer curiosity.

"Tricks you girls got to learn," Mercy told them as she demonstrated the art of stretching out her arms with her phone in one hand and her finger on the outside button. She had taken a picture of the five of them and the girls hadn't even realized it.

"Just remember to turn the flash off or some celebrities might take your phone or camera and smash it," Mercy explained.

"Good to know!" Jia told Mercy, using better English than any of them expected.

"You said that Camille is going to meet us in North Carolina in few days?" Jia asked Mercy.

"Camille and I play many piano duets in the past, she is amazing talent, she is my friend," Jia elaborated.

Mercy replied, "She has told me about your family's amazing experience and stories with the dragon. It is an honor to meet you finally."

The others didn't know a lot about Jia, just that her family was very connected in the shipping industry, and were curious to hear more about her.

"So you are from China?" Gretchen asked Jia. "My father likes China and Japan; he says that he receives a lot of inspiration from Asia in his designing."

Jia nodded as Gretchen spoke. "No, I am born in United States of America. My family's business is in China and many of my family is still there. I go and see them many times a year, but I like America the most," Jia replied nodding her head still.

"Why do you have such an obvious Mandarin accent if you are American?" Chloe inserted.

"Oh my family speaks Mandarin in my house so that I know how to speak English and Mandarin," Jia replied nodding approval.

"It helps my father too; he is still learning to speak Mandarin."

"So your mother is Asian and your father is American, that makes you American/ Asian with a Chinese family," Chloe decided.

Jia stopped nodding her head and smiling as she thought about that. Seeing that Jia was confused Chloe continued, "Zoe and I are American with French family, and Camille and Mercy are American with British family. Gretchen is German, Canadian, and American because she was born in Germany and her family came to the United States through Canada."

"This is a pretty complicated conversation for a road trip," Monique observed. She had come to the back of the coach to tell the girls that they would arrive within the hour.

"What is on your mind?" Ms. Monique asked Jia, seeing her confusion.

Jia cocked her head to the side and replied, "Chloe says that I am American Chinese but I think that I am Chinese/ American. I no understand what the difference is Madame?"

"My dear Jia, you are a beautiful mix of both Asia and American, like the perfect jade," Monique replied.

The girls were now looking at Chloe and Zoe's mother, wondering how that comment had anything to do with what they were talking about. Her daughters recognized the French in their mother as she demonstrated 'the art of distraction'.

Jia continued, "My family say that I should be happy and respect traditions of America but no forget that I am of Chinese descent too."

"My daughter means no disrespect, my darling. They have been confused themselves over the years and have spent much time understanding that we have all immigrated here from somewhere for more opportunities or to flee from unrest. Chloe especially has taken the idea of 'If you don't know where you come from you don't know where you are going' to heart," Monique explained.

Gretchen could see that Jia was a little frustrated. Her smile was gone and her eyes were near closed.

"I don't think the DM's care where we are from or what we call ourselves. They are what we need to be focusing on - when we are not having fun of course," Gretchen suggested.

"I am sorry. Gretchen is right, we are known better as the Others because we don't fit with any majority." Chloe carefully reached out to touch Jia's hand. Although she was not considered an adult yet, she could use her gifts to calm almost any situation with the slightest touch or breath.

"Ouch!" Chloe yelped as she brushed over Jia's hand.

Jia smirked a little as she raised her jade lizard eyes at Ms. Monique and the others.

"I see that you girls have learned the hard way not to touch a frustrated or angry dragon," Monique commented wryly.

"That is awesome. I can see now why you are with us!" Gretchen exclaimed. "I am not telling the boys; I will let them find out for themselves."

"I already knew," Mercy smirked.

Chloe and Zoe both started laughing.

"You're alright with us, and you can be from Iceland if you want to be."

"Iceland?" Jia replied, and then realizing the joke she joined their laughter.

The wee hours of the morning drew near, the time that most people called the Devil's Hour, but not those on the two motor coaches.

"I don't understand how sitting, talking and watching someone else drive can be so exhausting," Helen yawned. "Every time we arrive somewhere I feel like I need a nap."

"It is a good thing this time, my love," Atticus replied. "We all know that our hosts will be up early; however, they don't like to be woken up before it's time."

Atticus and Jonathan parked their coaches few feet away from each other.

"We are here but we will not be welcomed until the morning rooster wails," Senona announced.

On the other coach Jonathan explained the situation similarly and told everyone to grab a few hours of sleep. A big day lay ahead of them.

CHAPTER TWELVE

MOUNTAIN MEETINGS

It wasn't the sunbeams slipping through the cracks of the blinds; it wasn't the rushing water of the nearby creek or the sound of the rooster that woke the travelers. They were awakened by the shuffling of feet, tapping of fingers and loud whispers filling the quiet air of the mountain retreat.

"We are under attack!" Jeremy shouted to the other boys on the coach as he lifted one of the shades. Chase opened another shade, looking for danger.

"We need to arm ourselves guys," Jeremy announced. By now all the boys were up. They bounced from window to window, trying to see what all the commotion was about. They heard plenty of noise but saw nothing.

"I don't feel anyone outside of the coach," Ethan decided, yawning.

"Now that we are all up, I can promise you that we are not under attack. That is most certainly our welcoming committee, which I hope includes coffee." Helen made her way to the front of the coach.

"Don't you hear all that noise out there? Maybe you should have my dad go out before you, just in case there is danger," Jeremy warned.

Helen stopped and gave Jeremy a small smile. "I appreciate your concern, but I can assure you that there is nothing out there that wants to deal with me before I have my morning coffee."

Confused, Jeremy looked at Ethan.

"You don't even want to go there, Jeremy, she is right." Ethan said.

The sun was warm on Helen's face, the ground was soft and moist and the scent in the air was the fresh aroma of coffee.

"Good morning my lady, we are so happy that you and the little ones are here safely. I hope that your journey last night was undisturbed." A young woman pranced towards Helen. "I didn't forget."

"Coffee?" Helen sighed. "You are truly a goddess Nina."

"I hope our kids didn't make too much commotion while you slumbered. I told them they have to stay back at least 20 feet from the rolling guest houses. These kids today can be very creative in getting your attention."

Pausing from her coffee, Helen reassured her that they were no trouble, despite placing the boys in action mode. She was the first one out of the rolling guest house to prevent an immediate battle.

"It is so good to see you again!" Helen exclaimed while kissing the young woman on both cheeks. "We were extremely excited and surprised to hear that the elders had requested your assistance in this matter."

"We MUST assist in stopping the horrific crimes that these monsters..."

"No need to get all worked up again, Mother." The young woman was interrupted by an equally young man.

"Good morning to you and welcome," the young man said as he gave Helen a kiss on both cheeks. "I do hate to break up the love fest but I am going to have the lads move the cattle to the other pasture and your majestic but mammoth motor coaches are in their way." He looked pointedly at the coaches.

"I heard you loud and clear, you old Indian crow," Atticus shouted as he stepped off the coach and walked in the young man's direction. "Good to see you again lad, it's a good thing that you prefixed 'mammoth with majestic' when speaking of our motor coach!" Atticus and the young man collided with their arms open, hugging each other with such strength they lifted each other off the ground.

"It is a beauty, suffice it to say," the young man agreed.

"It is that, but not as majestic as these thousands of acres of nature that you and your family call home. I swear every time I come here it is just that much more beautiful than I last remember. Just like this young lady who lets you call her your wife." Atticus laughed as he reached over to hug her, too.

"You are still very charming and easy on the eyes yourself, Atticus," The young woman replied.

Anthony and the children were still in the motor coaches, waiting to be invited into the conversation. Jonathan had left in the tow vehicle earlier for his management conference in town.

"Girls, wait here for a minute while I introduce Monique and Avery to my friends," Anthony instructed the girls as Monique applied a final dash of lipstick.

As they stepped out and around the other coach, Luis cut in front of him with Senona.

"Luis, you big lug," Anthony protested while Luis smirked and pretended not to hear him.

"Good morning, my dears," Senona announced as she and Luis embraced them.

Anthony fell back with Monique and Avery while Luis wrestled with the young man and Senona gave them both kisses.

"So is that everyone at this point of your journey?" the young man asked Luis, knowing right well that Anthony and the others were only steps behind him.

"Very funny brother," Anthony chirped.

"You think I couldn't sense my own blood, Anthony?" the young man laughed.

Putting his hand out to shake, Anthony yanked his arm down and jumped on his back. Both fell to the ground laughing and wrangling.

"They look like a bunch of kids playing around on the ground," Chloe told Gretchen as they watched from the front window. Gretchen was perplexed. Her father didn't usually like to get dirty, and she had never seen him wrestle and play fight with others before.

"Yeah, I am a little confused," Gretchen admitted. "They look ridiculous."

"Enough messing around for right now." The young woman helped both men up off the ground.

"It is good to see you, Sis," Anthony said. "Please excuse me," Anthony added, remembering his companions. "This would be Monique and her husband Avery."

Avery stepped forward to shake hands and exchange greetings, as was the formal protocol for these meetings.

"Pleasure to meet you, Sir and Lady. I have heard much about you and your family. My wife Monique and I are honored to be your humble guests for the next week."

Monique straightened her hair one last time and waited.

"Welcome to you both. We have also heard much about you and your talents. Along with your two daughters, I believe?" The young woman shared a kiss on the cheeks with both of them.

"Speaking of the children, they are all a little too quiet. Unless yours are still sleeping?" The young woman smiled, knowing that they were all perched at the motor coach windows waiting to be announced.

With a hand gesture Senona and Monique had the children tumbling from the motor coaches. The young man whistled loudly and ten more children soon appeared.

The parents were quickly outnumbered by children.

"Welcome to our home," the young man announced to the children. "My name is Taj and this is my wife and children's mother, Nina."

"Let me see if I can figure out who is who here," Nina mused. Her face revealed little of her true age, hinted at only by the few strands of white highlighting her jet black hair. She placed her slender fingers on each child's head as she approached them.

"This one is easy because I have met you before, Gretchen," she announced. "It was when you were still a baby, but your blood and our blood runs the same path."

Nina gave her a kiss and stepped to the next child. "Jeremy and this must be Maximilian!"

"How did you know that?" Jeremy asked suspiciously.

"There are only a few of your kind left with that bone structure and muscle mass of a gargoyle. If you are like your mother, you won't let anyone stand between your brother and you!" she announced. Senona smiled at Jeremy as he postured a bit.

"You are too old to be part of the mission, and too young to be a parent, so I believe you are Tyson, son of Elijah and Alicia," Nina declared with a smile and kiss. "That would make this young man beside you your cousin Chase, who you are guardian over until your parents return from South Africa."

"Yes Madam, I am Chase," he replied softly.

"You are a lucky boy to have Tyson. He is a fine young warrior who will train you," Nina assured him, hugging them both.

"I can see and feel by your energy that you are my new friends' girls, Chloe and Zoe." Nina kissed them on the cheeks.

"How did you know that?" Zoe exclaimed, kissing Nina back.

"The energy from a Xana is pretty easy to detect. I am only a little surprised that you didn't receive more of your father's elven energy," Nina told her.

"That is really cool!" Chloe whispered to Ethan beside her.

Since it was just him and Mercy left and he was the only boy, Ethan wasn't surprised by Nina's naming.

"I have heard so many things about you Ethan. Mind you, I am one of those skeptics that was unsure if training a vampire child before his coming of age was appropriate. Apparently your father and mother knew that you were going to be amazing, so I welcome you to our home," Nina explained giving Ethan a kiss.

"Thank you Madame, I will not disappoint you," Ethan replied politely.

Last but not least Nina placed her hand on Mercy's shoulder.

"What a wild life you have lived already, Mercy. I think you better start writing down some of your stories. I guarantee Senona could turn them into a best seller someday."

"You may be right Miss Nina; I will," Mercy replied.

"I heard that your sister Camille is finishing up a brilliant soccer season and will be arriving later this week. I suppose you are in the same position as Tyson. You are going to look out for her while your father finishes his lecture series?" Nina asked.

Distracted by one of Nina's sons, Mercy stuttered a reply. "Yes, I am here to keep an eye on good looking young men."Everyone stared at her, and then started laughing. Mercy rolled her eyes. Realizing she had thought out loud, she waited for Nina's response.

"Well it shouldn't be hard to keep an eye on good looking young men or women with this Clann here!" she laughed, not wanting to embarrass Mercy any more than she had herself.

"As you can see, we have litter of children!" Nina exclaimed as one by one her children started to appear behind, beside and around her and Taj.

Max counted aloud as they appeared, "4,5 6..8,9,10," hesitating for a moment to see if any more were going to visualize.

"You have ten children?" Ethan said, thinking that three was a large family.

"Yes, Ethan we have ten children, which must be a lot for an only child to picture. Bearing children is not as difficult for our kind as it is for yours," Nina explained.

Ethan looked at his mother quizzically.

She was now finished with her coffee and he whisper-spoke to her, wondering what was so difficult about having him and why didn't they have more children. Helen merely smiled back and whispered, "I love you."

One thing seemed a little odd about Ms. Nina's children. Even though they had different shades of hair and eye color, the girls all looked alike and the boys the same.

"How come all your children kind of look the same?" Chloe asked.

"What are you talking about?" one of the girls chirped. "I am one inch taller than my sisters and I have larger lips than my sisters."

"If larger lips, you mean a bigger mouth, then you are correct," one of the other girls retorted as the rest of them started to snicker.

"I am definitely the strongest and best looking of us all!" another boy added.

The boy that had caught Mercy's eye replied, "Strongest in scent, definitely and best looking? Well, that would depend if I was in the room too."

Jeremy and Ethan snickered and Mercy blushed slightly.

"All right y'all, enough of the games. As you can imagine, with 30,000 acres to roam our children have plenty of time to work on their jokes. Maybe they could work on their chores too. While you are doing your chores you can introduce yourselves to your new friends." Taj looked up at the sun, which was rising quickly in the sky. He knew that trying to introduce all his children and explain their names and pronunciations would take more time than they had right now.

"Yes, I agree and our children will help them so we can park our majestic coaches," Atticus echoed, smiling at the children.

They ran off in groups, roughly ordered by age and gender.

"Nina, I can't tell you how happy we are to be here, even with all this chaos going on," Senona said holding the young woman's hand.

"Your babies are beautiful and radiant, just like you and Taj," Helen said extending her hand to hold Nina's other hand. "We are so sorry for your loss of your two children to these mirror men," Helen added.

"Thank you, my dear friends. It has been difficult these past months but we have all pressed on. We have faith that Giselle and

Haniahanka's lives were taken to unite us in stopping these beasts," Nina said somberly.

"How is the rest of your family holding up?" Senona asked.

"They have all gone through their own way of mourning, but I have to keep my eyes on Viho. He is a strong warrior like his father and will never lose sight of his prey. In this case though his prey doesn't have four legs or wings and will think nothing of turning his strength against him and us," Nina observed.

All three nodded their heads in agreement.

"This reminds me of when we were all young and believed the ancient ones worried too much about everything," Senona reflected.

"The only problem I have is that one of the ancient ones is now my husband." Helen smiled ruefully.

They all laughed and Senona added"...and we don't really look our age at all!"

"Some of us are doing a better job of that than others," Helen said as she lowered her head.

CHAPTER THIRTEEN

GAMES AND NAMES

It wasn't as if all the children didn't know one another at all. They had seen each other in the Serenity Channel on occasion, but it was sort of like seeing someone at the mall and then meeting them again and learning their name.

The morning flew by as they romped through the homestead and property.

After watering plants, picking off dead leaves, talking to the garden, filling up food bowls for the animals and washing down the horses, the girls finally sat down in the shade of a huge maple tree. They had chatted to one another as they worked, mostly about school, clothes, boys and their exciting summer adventure.

The boys caught up with them after

cleaning up cow manure, pig manure, tying up grape vines and playing with the dogs.

"Looks like you girls had the same idea as us," Jeremy said as he sat down under the large maple tree.

"You only think that you have done as much work as us," one of the girls sniffed. "But I guess it's alright for you to chill with us."

Uncertain, Jeremy thought it better to say nothing. After all, he was their guest and he had to sleep sometime. He didn't want crickets in his ears or whatever torture country girls would inflict on him.

The two youngest children ran off to the house as the others gathered around the tree for more conversation.

"Did we scare them off?" Gretchen asked.

"No. It is Kele and Aponi's chore to fetch us our mid-day meal after we have finished our morning duties. The twelve of us all have individual and partner duties that we perform," Nadine explained.

"Your names are unusual," Ethan blurted. "Or at least not as common as our names are," he amended, sensing Gretchen's disapproval. "What is the reason for your names?"

The oldest sister addressed this question like it was her responsibility.

"Our names reflect our personality and gifts in some sense. They are mostly tribal names from the east and west. For instance my name is 'Nadine', which means wise one. I do most of the public speaking on behalf of my brothers and sisters.

"Viho, my twin brother's name, means chief and he coordinates all plans," Nadine explained.

"More like bosses us around sometimes," Makya added.

"In your case you need to be bossed around since your head is so far up in clouds you don't seem to hear anything you are ever told the first time," Viho pointed out.

The brothers and sisters of the plantation laughed, including Makya as he threw some blades of grass at his older brother.

"Makya means eagle hunter and it is true that his mind is often lost in the clouds so we have to bring him back to earth regularly," Nadine explained.

"Sounds like my brother Max," Jeremy said, nudging Max with his shoulder.

Nadine continued to introduce the rest of her brothers and sisters. "Chogan is the third brother, whose name means black bird and his twin sister is Chepi which means fairy. You know Makya and his twin is Jaci, which means moon."

As she introduced them they each stood and did a little dance, chanting in an elemental language.

"Keme is our fifth brother and he is sneaky, his name means secret. Yoki is our fifth sister; her name means rain."

Just in time for introductions the two youngest came trotting down the slate walkway with two trays of food, one with fruit and the other with eggs, bacon, bread and pancakes.

"This is our youngest brother Kele which means squirrel and our sister Aponi, which by the way she moves should tell you that her..."

"Aponi means butterfly!" Max interrupted.

"Yes, her name means butterfly." Nadine laughed with the others.

Max was very excited that he knew what her name meant and he jumped up to help her with the fruit platter.

"That food looks so good, I could eat a horse," Jeremy informed them as he reached for a piece of bacon.

A murmur of disapproval froze his hand in mid-air.

"We must first bless the food and thank the earth spirits for providing us such great fruit. Next we must thank the beast for sharing its strength with us. All that is provided to us is nurtured by this land and water beneath us," Viho explained.

They formed a circle around the platters of food that rested upon huge logs near the trees where they were sitting. Viho started a chant while Nadine and the other brothers and sisters gave thanks for the food.

"All this food is from your land, rivers and lakes?" Chloe asked Nadine.

Nadine smiled proudly. "Yes all that we eat is provided from our ancestors' land. Our houses and buildings are built from the trees and clay. Most of our clothes we sew ourselves and the tools are even made here by our father, Viho and Chogan. Now eat - you will like everything."

Confused, Gretchen asked "Where are the plates and forks?"

"You eat with your hands. If it is too much for your hands, then it is too much for your belly at one time," Nadine explained.

"I am liking this trip so far!" Jeremy

exclaimed as him grabbed blueberries and bacon sandwiched in pancakes.

"That is really cool that you use everything, but what about money for buying things that you can't make?" Zoe asked.

"There is nothing that the farmer's markets won't buy from our family!" Chepi exclaimed. "We have the best meat, the best fruit, the best wine and the best catfish, bass, panfish and crappie that anyone has tasted."

No one was going to argue with someone with that much enthusiasm, especially while they were enjoying every bite of the breakfast they were eating.

"You not too hungry?" Jaci asked Ethan as he picked away at his food.

Ethan looked up from his hand of food, embarrassed. "It's not that. You said that there are twelve brothers and sisters, but you only gave us ten names."

A hush fell and Viho turned toward Ethan.

"You are correct Ethan; there are only ten of us left. Do you know that Ethan means enduring or one who has long life? This would be very appropriate for you, but it would not have been for my sister Giselle or brother Haniahanka. They were lured away from us when we made a journey to Winston- Salem last year. After our trade of fish and produce was over we asked our parents if we could go explore like other kids.

"It was then that we lost them. We searched for two days, and then we felt their souls missing." Viho took slow, steady breathes.

"One month passed by when Kele and Aponi tells Makya that they think that maybe they see our sister and brother coming down secret road but cannot get high to clouds to see. Makya soars high and fast and tells my sister Nadine, yes it is our brother and sister but they are weak. Father was fishing in the lake so Mother tells little ones to go tell him as she takes Nadine and me to help them home. As we get closer Mother is crying with joy and pain as she see's they are exhausted. "Then we see it, they tell us that you and some of the others have seen it too. Their eyes were like mirrors; there was no energy in their souls. I think maybe it is because they are tired so I hurry towards them, but with no warning little wolf lunges at me like he wanted to tear my head off, Giselle races towards Nadine with a large stone. I stop little wolf in flight and toss him at Giselle, knocking her down before she could strike my sister.

They did not stay down, they stood up as if nothing had happened and turned to Mother. Their eyes reflected the sun back at her. She had heard the stories of your mirror men, and how something evil steals their souls and makes them work as zombie slaves for them.

"She knew now that two of her children were possessed by this evil and she did not want them to suffer any longer. As my sister and brother turned again to attack Nadine and I our mother cried out as she unleashed the fire from inside her and destroyed them instantly. My sister and I were only a few feet away, we felt the heat from the flame, smelled the burning flesh and felt the pain in our Mother's heart as she fell to her knees. Father arrived moments later leaving a wake of debris behind him. He too knew there was nothing to be done. So that is why we were asked by the elders to assist in this plan to bring out these beasts."

"We are very sorry for the loss of your brother and sister. Yes, we all here have had some encounter with the mirror men," Ethan said darkly.

"We are pleased to have you all here, to embark on this mission but also to share our experiences with this thing," Nadine told them.

"We must now finish eating though because we have to exercise the cattle this afternoon," she added.

"You make the cattle in North Carolina do exercises; maybe I will use them to do my exercise!" Jeremy said as he lifted the large tree stumps that the food was sitting on up and over his head with one hand.

Jeremy knew he wasn't supposed to use his powers in public but no one would see them on 30,000 acres.

Yoki smiled at Jeremy and said, "You are really strong, but don't let it slip out of your hands."

With that, Yoki spun in a circle and created a water spout pointing right at the log that Jeremy was holding over his head. The log slipped from his hand and landed on his head. Chogan and Kele scurried around, not allowing one piece of food to touch the ground.

"You all are permitted to use your gifts anytime you want?" Gretchen asked.

"No, we are encouraged to use our gifts as often as we want as long as we feel they will not endanger the land or our family or ourselves," Makya answered as he soared up into the air.

Jeremy shook his head, saying "I am loving your place more and more by the minute. I can't wait till Camille gets here. She is always busting my butt for not being as discreet as I should be so I never get to do anything."

CHAPTER FOURTEEN

LIKE A ROCK STAR

"Camille, you need to finish packing!" Gregory repeated as she switched out clothes for the fourth time in two days.

"Lilith, I don't know what to pack for this vacation. I may have to climb a mountain, ride the rapids, dance at a ball or saddle a horse," Camille explained to her furry friend.

Lilith purred softly and slowly blinked her eyes, seeming to say 'you will make it all look easy and amazing.'

Camille had had some visions of the summer's activities, but she was still unable to lock into any of the DM's activities, which was becoming increasingly frustrating. She told Gretchen before she left that she didn't know if it was her not concentrating as well since her coming of age was nearing or if they were just that good at blocking even her. Gretchen reassured her that even the elders were having difficulty honing in on the mirror men and their puppet master, so she shouldn't be so hard on herself.

"My dear, the car will be here in 10 minutes to pick us up for the airport!" Gregory urged for the last time.

"I guess this load will have to do the trick," she sighed to Lilith as she tightened the latches on the two bags that she was permitted.

Camille texted Mercy that they were heading to the airport and would be arriving later that night. Technically, they were not allowed mobile devices at the plantation, but Mercy didn't always follow the rules.

Once at the airport, their limousine drove them behind the terminal and out to the middle of the runway.

"Where are we going?" Camille asked, concerned.

"We don't have to go through normal airport security; we are flying on a private plane, my dear," her father explained.

A beautiful white and black dual jet engine plane gleamed in the late afternoon sunlight. Her heart stuttered as she asked tentatively, "Is that your friend's plane?"

Looking across the tarmac, he replied "Yes, I believe that is John's plane."

"Oh yes, yes, yes!" Camille screamed as she pulled out her phone, checked in at the airport website and took several pictures of the plane, seemingly all at once.

Gregory apologized for his daughter's excitement to the car driver and tipped him as he unloaded their luggage. One of the air stewards took their bags and stowed them on the jet.

"It is alright sir; I would be pretty excited to fly on one of those sweet Gulfstream jets myself." The driver smiled. "Have a good flight."

Camille had already run up the flight stairs and was checking out the cabin like it was her first doll house. Gregory entered and the two large engines roared to life. A petite young woman closed the door behind him.

"Daddy, can you believe how amazing this plane is? It has leather everything, real wood and glass tables, three television monitors, a bar and that is just in the front."

Camille hadn't called her father Daddy much since she was a little girl. Usually, moments of extreme emotion triggered the endearment, which let Gregory know how impressed she was.

"It is pretty spectacular, as far as planes go. I am usually busy working or in meetings when I have flown in it before, so I may not have noticed," Gregory admitted.

The pilot appeared on a monitor and introduced himself. "Welcome aboard 'Amour III'. I am Fredrick and Wendy is your service provider. You are our only guests on the plane to Winston Salem, N.C. Feel free to wander the plane after we are airborne and at cruising altitude. Movies and games are available on the entertainment system.

"Wendy can provide additional services, such as refreshments and massage. Once we have our flight plan, I will come back to visit and answer any questions."

Camille and Gregory sat down in the large leather arm chairs and fastened their seat belts as the plane taxied to a far runway and waited for the all clear signal. Camille was mesmerized by the plane's beauty and glamour. Gregory had to remind her to breathe, so impatient was she for lift-off.

They began to taxi again, and then came to a sudden stop.

"I apologize for the delay," the captain

said. "Wendy, would you please come to the cockpit?"

Wendy gracefully left her seat and smiled reassuringly at Camille and Gregory as she headed to the cockpit. Moments later, she returned to the cabin and opened the plane door. A rolling stairway was visible outside. A teenager bounded up the steps, hopped into the cabin and dropped a guitar case and metallic suitcase on the floor.

"I will take those for you as we prepare for departure," Wendy offered, placing his gear into a closet and locking it.

The young man collapsed into the plush chair in front of Camille and her father. He fastened his seat belt and held onto the seat. The plane continued down the runway, picking up speed as the engines roared. Like a butterfly from a blossom, the plane lifted into the air. Rising in altitude, it made one pass over the city and river and resumed its flight plan.

"Sorry about the minor delay. What kind of flight would we have in a rock star plane like Amour if we didn't have a rock star on board?" Fredrick appeared on the monitor. "Apparently, this young man missed his flight and has to be at a concert tonight in New

York with some singer named Selena Gomez. Lucky for him, his agent heard that 'Amour III' was fueled and leaving for North Carolina, now continuing to New York City."

"Fortunately, John is a nice guy when it comes to lending out his plane," Wendy added. "It would have been tomorrow before the next flight left for New York, via Atlanta."

"Yes, miss, I feel very lucky indeed that I will make it there in time," the young man assured her.

Camille was still not sure how she felt about this change in plans. Only ten minutes ago her and her father were flying in a private jet alone and now some guy she didn't even know was on it, too. Even if he was cute, she admitted.

After Wendy told them it was safe to move around the cabin, the young man turned his chair towards Camille and Gregory. He seemed younger than Camille had thought, probably only sixteen or seventeen.

"I do apologize if I have hindered your flight experience in any way. My name is Chris. I'm not technically in the band, but I am part of Selena's lead dance team. The dancers are as much a part of her show as the music - or at least they want us to think that," Chris explained.

Still unconvinced, but intrigued by learning more about Selena Gomez, Camille introduced herself. "Hi, I am Camille. You know, this plane belongs to a friend of my father's. It's pretty awesome, right?"

"Crazy right; this plane is... off the chart!" Chris replied, hesitating a moment. He removed his sunglasses and rubbed his eyes, then popped out one of the ear buds plugged into his iPod.

"You know, this G650, which is made by Gulf Stream, has the largest cabin of any private aircraft. It's synonymous with the most luxurious and fastest non-commercial or military jet out there. It can travel 8000 miles at 0.85 Mach and has a top speed of 0.925 Mach. All the big names in the world of music, entertainment, and even Asian and Arab sheiks prefer to fly it. At $65 million dollars you definitely get what you pay for. You should if you have the money to buy or lease one of these babies," Chris explained earnestly.

Camille stared at him like he had lost his mind.

"Are you a walking Wikipedia or Gulf

Stream under cover sales representative?" Camille asked him.

Confused, he shrugged and replied, "I heard you say that you loved the plane, so I thought I would share some data that I knew."

Gregory took this opportunity to excuse himself and asked Wendy for a drink as he moved into the lounge area.

"I guess I just meant that it was really pretty, but that information is interesting, too. Thanks for sharing it with me, really. How do you know all that?" Camille asked.

"You spend enough time around something you want to know everything you can about it. That way, if I ever have to fly it, I'll at least have enough information to give it a good shot," Chris explained.

"Alright, I will give you that one. But why does a dancer for Selena Gomez carry around a guitar?" Camille probed.

"There are a few answers to that question." Chris laughed. "First, everyone thinks guys that carry guitars are cool!"

Camille giggled.

"Wait there is more," he insisted. "I have also been taking lessons from one of her band members between venues. Someday I would like to play in a band of my own as the lead guitarist.

"You look like a musician, too. I'll bet your know how it feels to have the energy and attention of a crowd all to yourself and not have to share it, don't you?"

Camille knew how that felt once, when she was younger and Mercy wasn't around. Then she could practice her gifts without interruption and have the elders' complete focus.

"Yes, she is an amazing pianist!" Gregory commented from the couch.

Camille turned around and stared daggers at her father. "Really, I thought you moved over there so you didn't have to listen to us talk about stuff."

"Well, you are an amazing pianist and I thought I would let your new friend know that," Gregory commented.

"Thank you sir, you must be very proud of your daughter," Chris replied politely.

Gregory just smiled and nodded his head in Chris and Camille's direction.

"So you do know how it feels. I want to know the same feeling someday. Don't get me wrong, dancing for amazing artists is really cool but I want that 'IT' factor someday. Maybe I will even have my own video game."

"Oh yeah, what would it be called?" Camille asked.

"CHRIS CROSS CONNECT!" He exclaimed. "Do you play video games? There is probably one in the media app that we could play on the flight right now if you want."

Camille laughed. "I'm not really into playing video games, but my friends can spend hours racing, playing and killing each other in those games, so I am obligated to watch sometimes."

"It can be a huge waste of time, but it can also be a great release of pressure," Chris added.

"So you know all about me. All I know about you is that you play piano, which you are sensational at according to your father, and you have crazy rich friends with G6 planes. Come on now, it is your turn to spill." Chris moved to the other luxurious leather chair beside Camille, rotating it towards her.

Camille thought carefully about the critical mission beginning this summer. She began to frame a response, cautious not to reveal to much personal information. On the other hand, it was just the three of them and he was cute. Apparently, he thought she was, too, as he leaned over the armchair towards her.

Before Camille had a chance to answer, Wendy appeared. "Miss Camille, there is only 45 minutes left in your flight; what can I get for you two to drink or eat?"

Camille was both thirsty and hungry but was not going to take a chance of getting food stuck in her teeth while talking with Chris.

"I think that I would like an orange juice mixed with one-third Sprite," she told Wendy.

"Oh my god, that's crazy!" Chris laughed. "I was going to ask her if she could make me the same thing. I like the Sprite first, then the orange juice so it mixes well in the glass."

Curious and excited by this coincidence, she agreed that was how she liked it as well.

"It reminds me of when I was just a little kid and my dad was still around. He would make my mom and him a mimosa every Sunday morning with Champagne and orange juice and make my sister and me one with Sprite or ginger ale." Chris explained.

Camille smiled at him and glanced at her father.

"My father made my sister and me one every time there was a special occasion so we could toast and party along with everyone else. Now I just order them when I need to feel special or celebrate something," Camille explained.

"Alright then, two virgin mimosas, with one third Sprite on the bottom of the high ball glass coming right up." Wendy hurried off.

"I don't mean to pry, but you said that your dad wasn't around? That's got to be hard," Camille said softly.

Chris adjusted the ear bud that was still lodged in his right ear, and took a deep breath.

"Yeah, in some ways it has been, but in other ways it has given me the freedom to let loose and do my own thing."

"So why did he leave and where did he go?" Camille pressed.

"My parents were young when they had me and still liked to party a lot. My mom and dad both were in the army so partying kind of went with the job. After my sister was born, my dad got deployed again but not my mom. It was hard on everyone but we managed; part of the job, you know.

"When he came back, he told her he had

been offered a job in the Middle East where he would work for a private security company. My mom and he argued about him getting out of the army early. She didn't want to raise her kids on foreign soil. The next day he was gone and I haven't seen him since." Chris shrugged.

"Here are your drinks," Wendy interrupted, handing them each a tall glass of bubbling orange juice.

"Thank you, Wendy," Camille replied.

"Yeah thanks; this looks perfect!" Chris added as they both took a sip.

"That had to really stink for all of you. I'm sorry," Camille continued when Wendy left.

"It did, but we moved on. Now you know even more about me and I am still waiting with only 30 minutes until you have to get off this sweet ride. You still haven't shared much about yourself," Chris reminded her.

She knew that she owed him something after listening to his family story. She also knew she certainly could not explain hers to him.

"Alright, well my story isn't much different than yours, except my mother is gone because we had to place her in a mental institution, probably for the rest of her life,"

Camille admitted. Her father looked up at her sharply, obviously biting his tongue.

"That's crazy, I don't mean like nuts but wow, ridiculous! You only hear about Hollywood types and lunatics going to mental hospitals. She wasn't one of them, was she?" Chris replied.

"No! She just lives in her own world," Camille explained. "It stinks because we don't get to hang out too much. She has never been to one of my soccer games or watched me swim, but she has heard me play piano."

"So you like soccer and swimming; there are four things I know about you now," Chris acknowledged.

"No, I love soccer like life; it is in my blood. I swim as much as I can because I love the water," Camille clarified. "The reason that I am late meeting my friends and getting to fly in this sick jet is because I am the captain of my soccer team and we made it to the playoffs. I wasn't about to let my team down and miss the play-offs for a trip."

Chris sipped on his drink and smiled at her over the glass with his deep dark eyes and tawny tousled hair.

"What?" Camille asked empathically.

Chris lowered the cup, licking the juice from his top lip before replying.

"I thought when I got on the plane that you were probably some spoiled rich girl who was going to have her nails touched up while talking on her cell phone during the whole flight about some totally useless reality drama while blowing me off. You are real, though and the issues and things you like are a lot like mine. Not to mention the passion for what you love is totally ridiculous!"

Chris reached out to hold Camille's hand as the plane made its final approach. Camille was tempted to use her gifts to learn more about him, but was afraid that would ruin the moment. She was enjoying this older boy giving her all his attention, and didn't want the illusion broken.

As the plane rolled to a stop, they shared a friendly hug as Wendy adjusted the stairs for their departure. A black limo was waiting just off the runway.

"Maybe I will see you again, or you can message me as cotocamille@gmail.com," Camille said shyly.

"One last question before you go," Chris asked. "How did the last two games of the soccer season turn out?"

Pleased, Camille replied, "We won one and tied one so we finished with PK's and we lost, placing second overall. It's all good though; it ended just like it was supposed to."

Gregory shook Chris's hand as they deplaned, wishing him a good flight and performance later that night.

Once they were in the car and leaving the airport, Camille texted Mercy "BAG<3/CUS/CD9."

"Honey, you are not supposed to be texting anyone," Gregory reprimanded her.

Camille groaned. "I am not texting Chris, I am texting Mercy. I told her I would let her know when we were here."

Gregory shook his head. "I can't figure out these coded letters you kids use to communicate with – but I suppose that is the point."

CHAPTER FIFTEEN

NOT DEAD, BY THE WAY!

"Follow me Camille!" "No, come with me!" A chorus of voices rang out.

"Really girls," Camille protested. "I have only been here for 24 hours and I was sleeping for 12 of them. What could be so urgent that I have to follow you both?"

"Easy there ladies, Camille hasn't gotten her hands dirty since she got here. She had to spill her guts to Mercy most of the day yesterday - that is, when she was not sleeping," Viho bellowed from a tree top.

Camille looked around while another voice chirped out, "You know that she is very close to her coming of age, sometimes priorities change."

Camille stood still trying to pick up on any clues as to which of the others was having fun at her expense.

"No way, it can't be you Viho?" Camille cried. "I was told that you and Nadine were captured or killed by the DM's."

Camille zeroed in on the branch where Viho had camouflaged his body.

Viho released himself from the branch and fell to the ground five feet from where Camille was standing.

"So does that mean that...," Camille began as Nadine stepped out from behind a rose bush.

"I suppose it does!" Nadine declared.

Nadine gave Camille a hug and Viho stepped into it, picking them both up off the ground.

Camille was so excited to see her two lifelong friends she had forgotten that the other girls wanted her attention as well.

"Looks like neither of us are going to get her attention now," Chloe said as she looked over at her sister.

Flattered, Camille assured them that it was great to see everyone. "I needed yesterday to decompress with Mercy, but I am here with you now.

"If I had known that we were going to be here at your place I would have tried to get here sooner and I would have come out of the motor coach yesterday. I can't believe it!"

"We didn't know that you were going to come either," Nadine said. "It wasn't until we were in town the other day and we were following what may have been a mirror man. We were working up a plan of escape should we need it, when your friend Gretchen told us that Camille would have a plan ready in a second. I asked her what Camille she was speaking of and she told me of the seer, mystic and soccer girl that would be here soon. It was later that I told Viho that you must be coming here too."

"Why did I hear that you two were dead?" Camille asked.

"We had not heard of us being dead, but yes, we lost Giselle and Haniahaka to these creatures you call mirror men," Viho said somberly. "I guess it is like the wind. When you tell a story, if the breeze carry very far then it picks up seeds and dirt," Viho added.

Camille nodded at Viho's explanation. She remembered Giselle and Haniahanka as being just a little younger than Nadine and Viho. She knew that losing a brother or sister in this family was devastating, since they cocooned only so often.

"I am so very sorry for your family's loss. I am happy that it was not you both," Camille added half heartedly. "We will all have to get caught up later; I suppose I need to be filled in on the current plan, what information you have retrieved and where everyone here has travelled from."

Mercy had made her way down to the crowd and took the lead on the introductions.

"The children around Nadine and Viho are their brothers and sisters and I am sure that they will introduce themselves to you later. You know Ethan, Jeremy, Gretchen, Max and you remember Chloe and Zoe, daughters of Countess Monique of Xanas realm and Lord Avery. This is Princess Jia of the Royal Dragon Clann and an amazing pianist and finally we have Chase who is..."

"My step brother; he and I are here to help Mercy as intermediates between you all and the elders." Tyson interrupted as he raced up behind Mercy.

Camille took the next few minutes to meet with everyone and get caught up on the latest happenings with each of them.

"Camille I have one very important question for you," Max asked. "Did you win the soccer championship?"

Unsurprised that no one knew the outcome, since there were no cell phones, no cable T.V. and no internet, she explained that it was a good series but they were not able to win it all.

"Next season we will work even harder. I don't know how you all can survive without a phone or internet out here," Camille thought aloud, changing the subject.

"We have better ways of connecting. We do have a piano that Jia has been teaching some of my sisters to play. I promised them a concert when I heard that you were coming," Nadine replied with a big smile.

Camille laughed. "I guess we will be going old school with communications. If your family has been doing it for hundreds of years then I suppose for one summer I can handle it, too. Now I want to hear all about the encounter that you all had with the DM's."

"You might want to hear about the DM's, but we want to hear about the dancing guy you met on the plane," Zoe announced wickedly.

Camille's eyes narrowed with disapproval and she turned to Ethan indignantly.

"DID YOU?"

"Before you put Ethan in his place for

interfering in your business, think about the fact that you texted Mercy. He is the only one that can receive messages, whether they are voice or digital," Gabriel's voice chastised.

"Then you spent the entire first day decompressing with your sister alone. You had to know that your friends were going to want to get the scoop too," Gabriel added, still not visible.

"Fine, I will tell you a little about the boy, but a girl has to have some secrets," Camille replied.

The girls clustered around, eager for gossip, while the boys scattered to find sticks to use as practice swords and spears.

After their gossip fest, Camille headed down to the river where her friends were practicing their gifts.

"You have got to see what I can do now!" Jeremy called out, seeing her approach. "It's really awesome that we can use our gifts for anything, even play."

Skeptical, Camille asked Ethan and Gretchen if she would have to take cover.

"Alright, what is it that you can do now that you couldn't do in the city?" Camille asked.

"Just watch." Jeremy took four steps into

the river, just deep enough to get the bottom of his shorts wet, and then splashed the water around and removed his baseball cap.

"I'm not interested in guessing," Camille commented. "Are you going to be chased by a fish like you were at Beltane that time?"

Jeremy ignored her. He took one more breath and placed his entire head into the river. Waiting impatiently, Camille and the others felt the ground beneath them start to shake and within seconds the river was flowing from both directions towards them, rising as it approached. The fountain grew higher and higher around Jeremy while the others watched and cheered him on.

Camille was pretty impressed by this mix of science and magic that Jeremy was performing. Her eyes started to roll back into her head as she caught a glimpse of a future situation.

With little warning Jeremy raised his head out of the water, heeded the vibration of the water and let it fall back into the river. As the last bit of water settled, Jeremy saw Camille returning from a trance. He cupped as much water in his hands as possible and tossed it all over Camille as she tried to dodge it.

"I saw that coming and I suppose I deserved

it." Camille snickered. "I am afraid that time I was too slow for my own good," she said as the water dripped from her hair.

"If you hadn't poked fun at me then I may not have done it, but I might still have." Jeremy laughed.

Camille was extremely impressed with Jeremy's interesting use of magic and controlled vibration. Only someone with a big mouth like Jeremy could perform that skill.

"I wasn't sure if you were going to suck up the entire river or blow bubbles, but that was pretty cool," Camille admitted. A disembodied voice announced,

"It's like water bending, which could come in handy. We have determined that the DM's are primarily communicating through computers and open electronic signals."

"Who's there?" Jeremy asked.

Ethan answered, "It's Gabriel, but he is not really here physically. HHHHHHHHe is keeping an eye on us through some metaphysical realm."

"Very good Ethan. Nice to see some of you are leaning to use your gifts with more control," Gabriel added.

Everyone grumbled, having a hard time

talking to air, let alone listening to air. Only Camille, Ethan, Nadine, Viho and Gretchen could see his projection.

"Listen, I like to see who I am talking with to make sure that it is not someone trying to mess with me," Jeremy explained to the general direction of Gabriel's voice.

Gabriel laughed at Jeremy's frustration. "Max, draw a picture of me in the sand," Gabriel instructed. "Make it nice."

Max squatted and began using a stick to create a version of the angel. Within a few minutes Max had completed his rendering of Gabriel.

"Help me up someone," Gabriel requested. "Looking up at your butts is not a great view."

Ethan reached down and touched the hand on Max's drawing. He began to pull towards him and the figure of Gabriel rose and stood on its own.

"Wow, now that is sick," Jeremy exclaimed. "Max you are really getting the hang of that drawing gift and Gabriel...I just don't know what to say, dude."

Gabriel stretched out his arms and legs then rolled his head back and forth a few times before continuing.

"From the feedback from different groups, it appears that the mirror men need to be near an energy source to communicate with one another. They seem to be able to store their energy for a limited amount of time by reaching a state of complete motionlessness," he reported.

"This doesn't explain how they initially were contacted or turned into these zombie-like creatures. It does, however, give the elders insight into how they track our whereabouts and communications."

"So that is why you don't want texting or any electronic communication," Camille replied. She dropped her head after realizing she had used her phone to contact Mercy.

"Yes, it's a theory we're working on. Apparently they were not able to intercept your message before Ethan did," Gabriel continued. "We do know that they are evolving faster than when you first encountered them a few years back. "Remember that as amazing as the world's technology is, it may be something as simple as water that could save the day. The basics of nature always win!"

Dirt and sand crumbled from Gabriel's avatar as he and his voice faded away.

Complete silence fell over the group.

Even the trees and water seemed to mute themselves as everyone thought about the danger of the situation.

"We knew that this issue was escalating and we were chosen for a reason, so we have to suck it up and focus on the goal," Ethan declared. "We will continue doing what we do best, out-thinking them and shutting them down for good.

"Remember, Camille, what you told us? The elders have many safe guards in place to protect us. We are special not just because we have our gifts but because we don't have all the pressures our parents have that distract them."

"Yeah and she already knew about the energy stuff," Jeremy added.

"Come on my friends, let us keep working on your gifts so none of us has the worries of being turned into a zombie creature," Viho suggested.

"Thanks for reminding me of our mission this summer," Camille told Ethan, placing her arm over his shoulder. "You maybe a few years younger than me but you have certainly become wise beyond your years. I can't wait to see what everyone else has been working on. That drawing thing of Max's was way cool."

"You haven't seen anything yet, and wait till you hear how Nadine and Viho and their family stay so young and fit," Ethan enthused.

CHAPTER SIXTEEN

CITY FORAYS

"Camille, Gretchen, Chloe, Zoe, Jia, you must get up out of bed now," Senona said as she shook the girls awake.

Opening her eyes just enough to see Jeremy's mom Gretchen mumbled, "Oh my goddess, it isn't even light enough to see you." She ghosted back out hoping that would buy her another hour's sleep.

"Alright girls since none of you are budging and you have to get up now, per orders from Nina and Taj, you have left me no choice," Senona apologized.

Closing her eyes and blowing through her lips with a gentle but firm force she produced a resonant sound so unbearable and deafening to their young ears that all five girls begged her to stop.

"Sorry Madame, for not listening to you

the first time," Gretchen apologized as she spoke the words without being able to hear them.

Happy to see that they were getting up out of their bunks, Senona retreated. As she opened the door Jeremy stood there shaking his head as he wiggled a finger in and out of his ear.

"Really Mom, did you have to use the siren's whistle? We were already out of bed and loading the truck for town. Now we can't hear anything either," Jeremy complained loudly. "Next time dump water on them, PLEASE."

"Sorry baby." Senona cupped her hands over both of his ears then removed them quickly.

Jeremy sighed, "Thanks, Mom."

Moments later Chloe stepped out of the coach. "Why do we have to get up so early and what is all the commotion about?"

"A storm hit the city yesterday morning and a number of our vendors are out of goods for market, so we need to fill as much as possible in the truck and deliver it quickly," Nadine explained.

"Alright but why are we all getting up? I

thought that was your family's thing," Chloe asked.

Nadine nodded. "Yes it is normally our thing but apparently the elders have information that there are a number of lost or homeless kids around that seem to be incoherent."

"That means that they are messed up, confused," Jeremy interjected.

"I know what incoherent means, dork," Chloe replied. "Which must mean the power went out. So these kids may be mirror men and they have had no way to communicate or retrieve energy."

"Sounds like this may be our opportunity to track one of the DM's," Camille said as she stepped out of the coach toward the truck.

"Maybe it is our opportunity to crush one of them in return for trying to attack us," Jeremy added.

"Hold up everyone," Atticus announced. He and Helen approached with several other parents. "We are only going to have six accompany Senona, Gregory and myself on this mission; we will monitor you children from nearby."

A low rumble started as the children argued over who was going and who was staying. They were tired of waiting and ready to track, attack or catch one of their targets.

"OK, OK we have already decided on who is going this time," Senona announced.

"Viho, Yoki, Camille, Gretchen, Ethan and Chloe will make this mission."

"I am not exactly questioning your decision, but I think I should be there to protect them just in case. I mean, I am the strongest here and can move fast if need be," Jeremy protested.

"We know what you are capable of and how you have been working on your gifts. However we need you here to protect our assets. We don't need you to be blowing off any of that steam on one of the mirror men before we are able to track them," Atticus explained.

"I guess I shouldn't have said that I was going to show them some serious smack down," Jeremy admitted to Zoe.

"Ya think?" Zoe replied, rolling her eyes. "I am happy that they are going to do the recon work, I'd much rather stay here and play with my powers and you boys."

Jeremy blushed as Zoe rubbed his shoulders and winked at him.

Atticus and Gregory took the six members

of the mission aside to explain the strategy laid out for them by the elders.

"Atticus and Lord Bashshar have communed and laid out some simple plans to gain trust and familiarity with the suspected mirror men," Gregory explained. "We will always be nearby in case any of you feel threatened. I am going to have Atticus explain the details while Senona and I prepare for travel."

Atticus led the six to sit under a tree for their briefing. "First and foremost, are we all aware of what to look for in their behavior and looks?" Atticus asked the younger ones.

They all agreed that they would know them to see them.

"That was the hardest part a few years ago and will continue to challenge us as they evolve, realizing that we are becoming familiar with them," Atticus explained. "Lord Bashshar is preparing two time and space ports for faster travel time since timing is critical. Senona will accompany the six of you while Gregory and I will arrive slightly before you to insure a clean passage.

"Once you arrive behind the marketplace with the truck of supplies, Senona will stay with the vendors as the rest of you seek out the mirror men. Once you have made contact with one, you will ask them if they need something to eat."

Atticus continued with the plan as everyone listened intently. Gregory returned as the sun started to break over the mountains.

"The truck is loaded and we don't want to miss our window of opportunity. Everything is loaded as normal, except we added one crate of hens to the back of the truck for a distraction if you have any problems when you arrive at the market," Taj informed Viho. "I know you will do well, you honor your brother and sister, my son."

"Yes father," Viho replied intently.

"It is going to be weird not having you with us," Ethan told Jeremy. "You better keep an eye on things till we get back."

"Hey, I got it covered; don't you guys worry about me. As a matter of fact, I have worked out a spell that will get us through chicken feeding without getting pecked anymore. Then I am going to see if Max will draw me something big that I can wrestle," Jeremy blustered.

Parents told the six to be safe and not to forget to communicate with each other, without cell phones or computers. They knew that they were going to be fine and they would see them for breakfast tomorrow.

"Everyone jump in; it is time to go," Helen instructed. Even though it was a big box truck with open sides, it was still a tight squeeze to get seven people in the front and back seats.

"Viho gets to drive?" Ethan exclaimed. "He is only 15 years old; I thought Ms. Senona was driving."

"Viho only looks fifteen, you dork. He is really more like 87 in human years," Gretchen explained.

"Oh yeah I forgot about their cocooning thing. Wow, 87 – you're pretty old Viho," Ethan decided.

"Not anywhere near as old as my parents - or your parents, for that matter," Viho teased Ethan back.

Ethan shrugged, bumping Camille in the head as the four in the back crowded on top of each other.

"Guess we really don't need seatbelts if we are going through a time and space port," Camille thought aloud.

"They didn't really help Dr. Who in the Tardis did they?" Ethan added.

"I didn't know you were a Dr. Who fan

Ethan. I love Dr. Who and his travels," Senona exclaimed. "This is certainly not the Tardis, which is huge inside."

With that thought in mind, Viho drove the truck into a bubble of energy that was only 100 feet in front of them. Everything seemed to slow down; they couldn't even hear each other speak as they were dragged effortlessly through the portal. Moments later Viho stepped on the brakes as they barreled into the city and towards a semi truck that was parked illegally. Senona chanted a quick phrase and the semi shifted to a legal parking spot.

"Wow, I never really get to see you in action Ms. Senona," Ethan exclaimed. "You are crazy fast with that magic stuff; Jeremy has to do it a few times."

"More often than not we end up on the wrong side of his casting!" Gretchen added.

They all laughed nervously, recognizing that this mission may have come to an abrupt ending if Senona wasn't with them.

Viho jumped from the truck as two young men ran over to help unload the goods.

"We are so pleased that your family was able to get this truck out to us in such short order," one young man told Viho. "My father has been running generators to keep the refrigerators cool all night; they are starting to get the power up in parts of the city but only 30% as of now."

Viho told the young men that he and his friends were going to see if anyone else needed help, so he would leave them the keys to move the truck if they were not back.

"No problem Viho, we will take care of everything. Not to rush," the other young man assured him.

With that, the six of them left the market area with Senona to fulfill their mission.

CHAPTER SEVENTEEN

TRACK OR BE TRACKED

"I never thought I would say that I liked grits but I was so hungry I could have eaten a third bowl," Camille sighed.

They had made their way into the heart of the city where a local homeless group had set up a portable dinner in a park for everyone. The best part of the early morning was spent checking out the damage the storm had caused and assisting people with getting in and out of their homes. As they worked their way to the city center, they scoped out the different groups of people which had assembled around the park. If they found their targets in poor condition, befriending them would be easier before the entire city's power was back on line.

Camille noticed several kids wandering around aimlessly.

"Listen guys, I think that if I shift into a stray cat and Gretchen stays close in ghost form I may have a better chance of finding out if those are mirror men or not," Camille explained looking in their direction.

Senona agreed, suggesting that Camille may want Ethan to walk over with them and try to pick up any internal conversations with his whisper-speak skills.

"I will have Atticus keep watch from a distance. Viho, Yoki and Chloe stick with me so we can continue observing others and insure your safety," Senona explained.

Ethan packed up some food in a bag from one of the tables and walked cautiously in the direction of the kids. He half expected them to start moving away from him but they didn't. They just stood staring at him, rocking back and forth as if unaware of their own legs.

"Hey guys, I was wondering if you wanted some food," Ethan offered softly. "It's free, and it is pretty good even if they don't have smoothie peanut butter, which I like."

Ethan was disturbed by the emptiness of their thoughts. These kids were acting like movie zombies. They were swaying back and forth, lifting their heads then allowing them to fall for no reason. As they shuffled cautiously towards him their eyes tracked random movements but did not focus.

They didn't seem much different than him; much like that girl Emily that he met in the square last month. They certainly didn't seem to be as aggressive as the ones that he had originally encountered at the Beltane festival.

Ethan saw Camille, or rather a scruffy-looking cat, perched on a nearby park bench.

He started in her direction, then stopped and whispered "Is that you?"

Camille purred while nodding her head.

Ethan still hadn't figured out how she could shift into these other creatures or what happened to her clothes. Maybe she was naked.

"I am NOT naked," Camille hissed. "Remember, I can hear your thoughts, too."

Embarrassed, Ethan looked intently at his feet.

"Come sit on the bench with us," Gretchen whispered directly in Ethan's ear. "They may respond better if you are sitting down. Oh yeah and eat a bite or two of food so they don't think it's a trick."

Ethan moved to the bench and sat

down; he placed the food beside him and encouraged them to share.

"I can't eat all of this and I don't want it to go to waste," Ethan taunted Camille and Gretchen as he placed a cracker in a pod of peanut butter.

Camille rubbed up against him, so Ethan naturally rubbed her head and ears like he would with Alix. Camille in return snatched a cracker from the bag and started licking it before tearing it into pieces.

This caught the attention of one of the kids and they smiled and laughed a little.

"I guess the kitty is hungry too," Ethan said looking at the confused boy.

The boy came a little closer; Ethan took out some more crackers and some fruit. Another approached after the first boy took an apple and bit into it. He sat down on the bench and took some crackers in one hand and proceeded to pet Camille with the other.

"You are doing great," Ethan heard his father tell him. Ethan smiled as he worked on detecting any signal that the DM's might be using to communicate.

Invisible, Gretchen looked to see if there was some hook up or port that they needed to download or upload power or information.

She was able to observe their figures from close range but could not touch them for fear of detection.

"Over here, look over here," Yoki cried out from across the park. Yoki had found two young kids lying on the ground behind some bushes.

"Are they dead?" Chloe asked with some suspicion.

Viho approached the boy and girl. He could hear a faint breath and the beat of a heart. "They are alive but barely," Viho stated calmly.

Senona bent down for a closer examination. "It is apparent that they have been beaten up pretty badly," Senona observed.

Bruises and swelling marred their faces and lacerations covered their arms, but their hands showed no evidence of fighting back.

"Why wouldn't they fight back?" Chloe wondered.

"I am not sure but we have to help them quickly or they may not make it," Senona announced worriedly as she placed her hand on the girl's forehead. Senona looked around for anything that she could use to design a concoction to give them some strength and energy. There was very little available since the storm had damaged so much in its wake.

"Chloe, I am going to have to ask you for a huge favor," Senona explained. "I need to take some of your energy and place it in this crystal."

"Madame, I can give you some," Yoki offered. "Chloe is so small, if we have any problems getting out of here we are all going to need everything we have."

"That little girl has a very special gift of receiving and storing energy," Senona explained. "I wouldn't let her size fool you."

Chloe held Yoki's hand and said, "You are such a sweet boy for offering yourself Yoki, but she is right. I have much more energy stored than you can ever imagine."

"This may take a while, since they are battered," Senona explained. "Viho, I will need you and Yoki to stand watch but be very cautious."

The brothers knew that meant that they would have to stand guard as anything but themselves. Yoki's muscles started to contract and his body started to shake as if he were going into a seizure. His body seemed to fall away as an eagle bolted from his clothes.

"AWESOME, freaking awesome!" was all Chloe could think to say.

Viho was the next to change. He used his body as a blind for Senona and Chloe by turning himself into a huge flowering bush.

"Wow, I never knew what was so awesome about these lepidodryads," Chloe exclaimed to Senona. "I knew that they stayed young by cocooning every so many years like butterflies and the dryads I have met in the past were pretty cool but blended together they are freaking AWESOME!"

"They are certainly a very special and rare family my love. However let's focus on task of saving these young ones and maybe they will have some answers to the question of who is trying to destroy us," Senona explained, gathering Chloe's focus.

"Yes Madame, it is just that those boys are so hot and exciting," Chloe sighed.

"Yes they are," Senona agreed, amused, "but now channel that energy into this amethyst."

Chloe sat in yoga Buddha position with the crystal in her hands cupped in her lap. Unmoving, she focused her energy into the amethyst. After thirty minutes, the crystal started to glow. She handed it to Senona to place in the arch of the boy's foot.

"This is a good start my dear," Senona said approvingly. "I will start with feet and pull earth energy and cosmic energy through the crown. It should be enough to get them mobile."

Chloe exhaled, and turned to see Yoki and Viho still standing guard. She smiled as prettily as she could at the flowering hawthorn bush and batted her eyes.

Ethan was busy talking to a few of the stray kids. They were becoming a bit more mobile as the sun came out and the day passed.

"Isn't this the nicest and prettiest cat you have ever seen?" one of the girls asked Ethan. "Is it yours?"

Ethan carefully chose his words. "I think it is a she, and she is not technically mine but she has been following me around," Ethan replied. "She is a little scruffy but she does seem to be well mannered for a cat." Ethan rubbed Camille's back and pulled gently on her tail.

"If she is not yours, than I think I will make her mine," the girl replied. "She probably wouldn't want a boy to have her anyway."

Oh boy, Ethan thought just as Gretchen weighed in from inside his head.

"You had better think of something fast or I know Camille is going to do something and you are not going to like it," Gretchen warned.

Ethan did not want to be on the other end of Camille's frustration, especially in cat form; he got enough of that from Daisy at home.

"I will think of something," Ethan told Gretchen. "Have you seen anything that could be out of the normal on or around the kids?"

"Nothing out of the norm, except that they seem to be becoming a little more aggressive. Those two boys over there are going to kill each other over some dumb video game that they are playing on a tablet. Really, you boys and your video games!"

"Hey I don't want to kill anyone but creatures and zombies on the video games that I play," Ethan protested.

"Hey you, do you hear me?" The girl was shaking Ethan's shoulder. "You hear me, I am going to take the cat, and I think she likes me best. What's up? You are staring out in space like you are staring at aliens," the girl said challengingly.

Ethan shook his head, explaining that it had been a long night and morning and he was just tired.

"OK, whatever," the girl replied. "Why don't you come with us? We are going up north to see Mother."

"We'd better be careful now," Ethan whispered to Gretchen and Camille. "They are becoming more aware, and we can't let them figure us out."

Atticus had noticed that the kids were feeling better; he could feel their energy starting to spike.

"This is similar to when I was attacked before in Asia," Atticus warned his son.

Ethan realized he had to get this girl to give up Camille and get out of the growing number of kids in the crowd.

"Hey, I think I see a rash on the cat's belly; it probably has fleas," Ethan explained to the girl. "If you want to give me your mother's address I could have the cat treated and then bring her up to you later this summer."

The girl looked at the Camille and back Ethan; Camille vigorously scratched her head with her back foot. The girl seemed to lose interest in the cat. She and some of the other kids started looking across the park to a section fairly dense with trees and bushes.

Atticus warned Ethan that Senona and the others were over there, working with some injured quotidians.

"Just hang in there for a few more minutes, son," Atticus told Ethan. "Keep the focus on you. We have to let Senona and the others finish and get out of there."

Ethan thought for a minute. "I want to play that game you are playing! I want to play that game you have!" Ethan shouted over at the two boys Gretchen had noticed. He ran towards them, which seemed to work as a distraction.

Camille jumped down from the bench and ran towards Senona and others. Gretchen followed.

"I want to play that game too," Ethan exclaimed in a louder voice now.

"You can't play it, it is mine and no one is going to touch my game," the one boy screamed at Ethan.

"Why do you have to be like that?" Ethan said as he reached for the game. A crowd of kids started to form.

"I sure hope Ethan knows what he is doing," Gretchen said when she reached Senona.

Ethan tried to grab the game, whisper-speaking his father to determine if everyone was safe. Atticus assured him that they were and it was time to leave.

By this time, there were three other boys and a girl that wanted to play the game and they were getting pretty rough.

For a moment, Ethan wished that Jeremy was with him. They could wipe out the entire group together. But that wasn't an option and wasn't his mission, anyway. He had to find a way to slip away unnoticed.

As Ethan considered his options, a familiar sound filtered through the noise of the arguing children. 'Da,da de,de, da,da,de, de,da,da' - an ice cream truck was coming down the road and into the park. All the kids stopped, recognizing the music of hot summer day ice cream treats getting closer.

"Ice cream, ice cream," one kid shouted out. "We all scream for ice cream!"

All of a sudden all the kids that were fighting minutes ago were singing ice cream songs and watching as the truck got closer.

Ethan couldn't believe his luck. The truck had distracted the kids and he prepared for his getaway.

The truck stopped within feet of the kids,

the music blasting out from a loud speaker on the roof. The kids pushed up to the side of the truck, anticipating the doors opening to deliver ice cream. Ethan waited, curious who he had to thank for this break. When the doors flung open, standing front and center in the truck was Camille's father.

"Alright kids what will it be today? Everything is free," Gregory announced merrily.

Ethan laughed at the paper hat and loose jacket on Camille's father, who was always so proper in his attire. With all the children clamoring for ice cream, Ethan turned to slip away.

A familiar face caught the corner of his eye. It was Emily. She saw him too and smiled. This wasn't the time or place for their next encounter. She waved goodbye as Ethan leaped into the trees and followed his dad's voice to safety.

"We are so glad you are safe," Senona greeted Ethan.

"Question, who are they?" Ethan asked with great curiosity, looking at the bedraggled kids next to Senona.

"They were attacked before the storm by the mirror men and were almost dead," Yoki explained. "Madame and Chloe saved them.

We are going to take them with us till they are stronger and get more information from them."

"So it looks like your group got more intel than we thought and we got plenty of information, so we need to report it to the elders," Camille said.

"Yes, we do need to take this information to the elders," Gregory agreed as he walked in on the conversation.

Ethan started to smirk.

"Thank you for the distraction sir," Ethan said. "I didn't expect an ice cream truck when I was working out my exit strategy."

"What is so funny?" Gretchen asked. "I think today was anything but."

"Nothing much and everything," Ethan shrugged.

"Well spill, Mr. Funnybones," Camille added.

"I never thought that securing info on the DM's would have me rubbing your ears and tail for hours and then turning around to see your father in an ice cream man's uniform!"

Everyone laughed, breaking the tension from the day they just had.

"That is why we spend so much time teaching each of you how to use your gifts properly," Gregory piped in. "But sometimes you have to go old school and jack an ice cream truck instead of escalating a conflict."

Atticus smiled and raised an eyebrow. "Old school? I hardly remember when it was that simple."

"That's because you are ANCIENT school," Gregory replied.

"Come on, let's blow," Viho announced to the group.

"Did you just say 'let's blow'?" Chloe asked Viho. "Wow, I am learning plenty about your family. Maybe you're not as square as I thought you were. OK, let's blow!"

Ethan fell behind the rest with Camille and Gretchen and told them about seeing Emily in the group as he was leaving.

"Do you think we should be concerned about that or is it just coincidence?" Gretchen asked.

"I don't think there are any coincidences when it comes to the DM's," Camille replied.

CHAPTER EIGHTEEN

BRAINS

"That sounds ridiculous," Jeremy exclaimed after hearing out the events in the city. "I probably would have gone garg-crazy on those DM's if they were surrounding me! I guess I could have whirled up a little magical distraction too. I probably should have used the magic, but I probably would have garged out."

"Still working though your demons?" Gretchen asked Jeremy as she sat down with the others.

"It's hard," Jeremy told her. "I know I am supposed to learn to be more diplomatic, like talk things out and think things through. But honestly, I would rather just beat the snot out of the bad guys and save my smooth talking for the ladies."

"Oh please don't go there; I don't want to

throw up my breakfast," Gretchen muttered. "Oh and please Mr. Smooth talker, if you take your shirt off one more time to show me or anyone else your abs, I am going to spray paint clothes on you!"

Gretchen could see that Jeremy was thinking the whole spray painted clothes was a good idea.

"That was a pretty intense day. I hope that Mr. Gregory, Lord Atticus and Madame Senona get some useful info out of those two kids we saved," Chloe told the others.

"I hope so too, after what you guys went through," Nadine replied.

"I learned a lot about your family though," Chloe told Nadine. "You have the most amazing brothers, so powerful, delicate and sexy!"

"Sexy, what haven't you shared with me sis?" Zoe asked.

"Thank you Chloe, I feel that they are amazing too. I don't know about the sexy part but I will take your word for it," Nadine replied.

"No, really," Zoe insisted. "Sexy how?"

"I see now why you lepidodryads are so secretive and protected way out here," Chloe said. "You guys are one of a kind."

"We thank you for your kind words but we also wish you don't speak of us to others please," Viho replied.

"Yeah I get it, sure. I don't think anyone would understand or believe me if I did," Chloe told Viho and his family.

"I couldn't see anything that would be a link or a source for them to send or receive messages with one another," Gretchen interrupted, changing the subject. "However, once they started getting more coherent it was obvious that they were communicating somehow."

"I agree," Camille stated. "I could feel a change in the energy of the girl that wanted to take me home. Her touch had some kind of current or signal in it that changed with her level of interest."

"I noticed that their eyes were not so glossed over like the first ones that we encountered at the festival or even Emily's," Ethan added. "Maybe they found out that we could see that and figured out a way to change it."

"Were you scared very much?" Jia asked hesitantly. "You must have not known what could happen. Do you think they know what you are too?"

Ethan and Gretchen looked at Camille, while Chloe and Yoki looked at Viho to answer Jia.

"I feel we were all maybe a little uneasy at first, but we have had plenty of training and had elders not far off to assist us," Camille replied. "Would you agree?" Camille said looking over at Viho.

"Yes, I agree," Viho replied. "You have to remember that we are both the prey and the hunter..."

"What my brother is trying to say is this: 'If you want to know the hunter you study his prey.' For instance if you want to know who is eating the chickens you have to first know the chicken," Nadine explained.

"I get it," Jeremy shouted. "So you would have to know how heavy the chicken is, if it cries out when it is eaten, does it put up a fight. So when you answer these questions you know how big, how strong, how fast and how hungry the hunter was."

Everyone stared at Jeremy. It wasn't like him to think things through that much and have the right answer.

"Impressive, strong and smart," Zoe said.

Jeremy puffed up his chest a little, but didn't reply.

"Yes, you are right," Nadine replied. "The problem is that we are both the hunter and the prey and this means that we have to examine our own strengths and weaknesses and figure out which of us are going to be higher on the prey list for the hunter. We in turn have to figure out which of the DM's are higher on our prey list too."

"I don't know about everyone else but this is hurting my head," Chase announced. "I am going to find Tyson and ask him what he thinks."

Gabriel and Atticus had been working on extracting information from the two kids that were brought back. They were both good at getting answers; however these kids didn't have a lot to share with them.

"It is as if their minds have been wiped clean," Atticus said to Gabriel as he wiped a drop of blood from his chin.

"I agree, that is what it seems like. However it has been my experience that if it ever was in there then I can find it one way or another," Gabriel replied. "I am going to speak with Gregory; maybe he has something that we can use to loosen those memories."

Helen and Senona knocked on the door

of the room where the kids were being questioned. Atticus opened the door and slipped out.

"They are only children," Helen reminded her husband as she wiped a smear of blood from his neck.

"I am being gentle, and Gabriel has them in a trance so they won't remember much, if anything," Atticus assured her. "I told him if he taught me how to create those trances then he wouldn't have to waste his time with us."

"I am sure he laughed at you again," Helen replied as Atticus smiled.

"We wanted to let you know that we have been monitoring the children this morning and they are amazing," Helen reported.

Senona agreed, saying "They have been working through yesterday's events, warning the other children of their findings and even teaching each other the art of war! I couldn't be happier with how much they have grown over the past few years."

"I am really pleased to hear they are taking this all very seriously, because these mirror men are very well organized," Atticus explained.

"Those are just kids, and they were beaten within inches of their lives. I can't imagine that they were or are mirror men," Senona exclaimed.

Atticus shook his head. "They were or are mirror men, and Gabriel has confirmed the technology has shut down part of their memory."

Senona herself was a powerful witch, an astonishing teacher and student in the art of magic and could channel energy through almost any creature. She stared longingly at Atticus.

"How is Gabriel able to access the brains of these two little kids and figure out that something or someone is deleting or blocking their memories?" she asked.

"I have read much on recent studies of the brain," Helen stated. "Scientists have discovered that different parts of the brain store different functions. Remember that article that you wrote on methylphenidate and how they use it to modify the amount of the neurotransmitter dopamine?"

Senona nodded as she recalled the article.

"Alright, so what Gabriel is doing is using his energy to work his way into the temporal lobe and prefrontal cortex where we store general knowledge, facts, recent memories and new data. From what Atticus is explaining, there is NO action in those areas at all and there should always be activity there," Helen explained.

Atticus smiled and nodded at her.

"Alright so Gabriel has done his angelic brain scan thingy and there is something wrong with those two," Senona said, pausing for a moment. "Oh my lady, what have I done? First saving them with our children's energy, and then bringing these infected kids back to our friend's farm."

Senona was beside herself in pain and frustration.

"I was sure that they were just human children that had been attacked by mirror men. I thought when they recovered we would get useful information from them, which would assist us in tracking and stopping this insanity. I am worried. If I can't tell the difference, then how can our children?" Senona added desperately.

"Can they hurt our children by being here?"

"My dear, none of us know what science or magic they are using to seduce our children," Helen comforted her friend. "Our children are very smart and well trained; they will make us proud."

Nina, Taj and Gregory approached hurriedly.

"I have news from Gabriel," Gregory informed the others seriously. "The elders want the two visitors disposed of immediately, and have asked Atticus and Luis to take care of it. They want us to leave Nina and Taj's land tonight; we are not to compromise their sacred land. You will be heading to the mountain dwellers in Virginia."

"We will be leaving for the mountain dwellers, but are you not joining us?" Senona asked.

"I have to attend a meeting out of the country, at which point I have been instructed to meet with other families and deconstruct their findings of this plague," Gregory informed her.

"Mercy will be able to continue the trip - if that is alright with her boss!" Gregory added, knowing that Senona would agree.

"Of course she can stay. I can give her plenty to write and edit while the children are doing their thing," Senona said with a smile.

Helen stepped aside with Atticus for

a moment while Nina, Taj and Monique gathered up the two kids' belongings.

"My dear, I am not sure of Lord Bashshar's decision to have us enter the dens of the Grottoasrais clans and the Appalachian tribes after our last encounter with them," Helen said, concerned.

Atticus admitted his similar misgivings; however, Lord Bashshar informed him that it was written and all would be as it should. There was no arguing the decisions laid down by the elders.

"Rest easy, my love. I need to inform Luis of our mission when he returns from his horseback ride with the children." Atticus chuckled at the thought of Luis' huge figure on a 16-hand horse.

"If I remember correctly, you enjoyed riding horses bareback at one time," Helen replied. "It is good that Luis still enjoys that connection."

"I will inform Mercy and Tyson of the plan before I leave. They can make sure that the children are prepared," Gregory told the others. He hugged and kissed Nina and Taj, thanking them for their hospitality as they returned with the kids' belongings.

CHAPTER NINETEEN

TIME TO RUN

"I don't know which would be funnier, you riding that horse or the thought of the horse riding you," Atticus told Luis as he returned from his ride with the children to the lake.

"You're jealous that they all like me," Luis replied, thinking of how many times Atticus had spooked a horse and been thrown.

Maybe so, Atticus thought as he shook his head. Horses were very sensitive to Atticus' energy. Perhaps they sensed the many times he had resorted to feeding from them during hard times.

"Whoa," Viho settled his horse as he approached Atticus. "I am sorry, sir. He is not usually this skittish around strangers."

"I rest my case," Luis crowed as he dismounted and walked his horse to the stables. "I may not be able to read your mind but I know you well enough to know what you are thinking."

"Perhaps. Right now, however, you and I have some business to attend to," Atticus explained.

Viho took Luis' mount as Atticus and Luis headed back to the house. They passed Mercy and Tyson, who had just returned with the other riders.

"We must complete our business here," Atticus informed them. "Insure that the children know that we will be leaving as night falls."

Mercy and Tyson both nodded their heads. "Yes sir, they will be ready."

"Once your horses are cooled down, saddles stored and bridles returned, we need to speak to everyone," Tyson announced to the excited riders.

Tyson and Mercy smiled as they listened to the others' horse stories. Some were talking about how their horse was galloping so fast that they were leaving the ground, still others were explaining how their horse knew exactly where to go and jumped everything that got in their way.

"I like to ride horses, and I remember telling similar stories after my first ride," Tyson reflected. "What about you?"

Mercy paused, trying to think of the last time she rode a horse.

"Not that I don't like riding horses, it's just that we have a lot of similar characteristics which makes it a little awkward to control the horse," Mercy explained.

"I didn't think about that," Tyson replied, remembering that her father was a *pooka* and her mother a forest nymph.

"I suppose there is something to be said about being old enough to drive," Tyson added. "Cars don't know what we are or where we came from."

Mercy agreed. The children gathered quickly, curious and anxious. Camille sensed by Mercy's posture that she had something serious to say. She had already had a vision of some dwellings in a mountain and the climb up to them.

"So are you going to tell us that we are leaving here soon?" Camille asked.

A low grumbling came from the others as Chloe said, "Please tell us that isn't the case. We are all having a great time and enjoying our hosts' hospitality."

"Camille is right," Mercy replied. "As we speak Ethan and Jeremy's fathers are removing those kids we brought back from the city. They have informed us that we will be moving out as the sun sets."

The rumble got a little louder as the children shook their heads in complaint.

"Mercy, there must be a way that we can stay for just a few days longer," Gretchen protested.

"I have enjoyed my stay here as well; however the elders have set in motion our next plan," Mercy explained.

"What if the elders gave us this night to say our goodbyes and we leave first thing in the morning?" Ethan suggested. He realized, too late, that his father preferred to drive at night.

"There is more to it than that," Tyson explained. "The two kids you brought back yesterday were infected with the mirror men stuff. They are currently being disposed of, like Mercy told you. If somehow they were tracked here, then this whole farm and community could be in jeopardy."

Silence fall over the group. The thought of their friends losing everything to the mirror men because of them hit a sour chord.

"Mercy didn't want your last few hours here to be a downer, but I thought if you knew the danger you would understand better," Tyson said as he grabbed Mercy's hand.

"Tyson is right. I think the elders have a plan as long as we leave tonight," Mercy assured them.

"Agreed," Camille said. "I don't have anything to pack because it is all in the motor coach. So the way I see it, we still have 4 hours to talk and work on magic."

"Me too." Max added, "I don't want bad things to come here and hurt my friends." Max looked shyly at his new friends Kele and Aponi.

"Do we know where they want us to go next?" Jia asked.

"No, we were not given that information, probably for our own safety," Mercy replied.

"Anywhere we go has to be better than this lame place with no computers, no video games and no television," Chase commented.

Everyone looked at him as if he were naked.

"What! It's true, all of you have thought that while we have been here," Chase snapped.

"Alright, I will admit that I have thought it," Chloe admitted. "But now that I have been here for a while, and after seeing what we saw yesterday, I am kind of liking this back woods thing. No offense to your family!" Chloe was quick to add.

"I wasn't sure how I felt at first, either. I do miss instant information on the net; however my gifts are stronger and I am more aware with fewer distractions," Camille added.

"Keep telling yourself that," Chase snorted as he walked away.

"Come back here and apologize for your rudeness," Tyson demanded.

Chase didn't even turn around as he kept walking. Everyone else froze as they watched Tyson morph into his vampire form. He was a foot taller, with eyes as blue as the sky. His shoulders spread so wide that his shirt ripped. Tyson leapt towards Chase, landing 50 feet away and only inches from Chase's face.

"What are you going to do, bite me? Tear my skin off? Or tell Uncle and Auntie?" Chase snickered. "I am not scared of you or anyone here or out there for that matter," he added.

Tyson grabbed him and lunged back to the group with Chase in tow. Chase was shaking as Tyson held his shoulder tightly with one hand.

"Show some respect to our hosts, if not to me," Tyson demanded.

"Careful Tyson, you are hurting him," Mercy cautioned.

Camille knew that Tyson was not hurting Chase. She could see that his grip was that of support rather than submission.

"That is pretty sneaky and sad," Ethan told Chase after reading his thoughts.

"I agree," added Camille.

A few of the group were feeling bad for Chase. Jia had smoke coming from her nose, and Jeremy was feeling the garg coming on.

"What is sneaky and sad?" Max asked.

"Tell them," Tyson instructed Ethan.

Ethan looked at Camille for help, because he felt his anger rising.

"Chase has no respect for any of us," she said slowly. "He thinks that we are all weak and that our gifts are a joke in this day and age. The reason that he is shaking is not that he is scared; he is trying to awaken his gifts so that he can get away from us. But because he has denied them he cannot reach them, let alone control them like us."

Chase stopped shaking and dropped his head.

"None of you know what I have gone through with the loss of my parents," Chase spat. "You would feel the same way if you were in my shoes."

"I know we don't know you that well or you us. But we all have some issues with our families," Camille explained. "We have decided to work on strengthening our gifts before any other activity. We are all here because the elders feel that we have something special to offer. These DM's have been stealing our friends and family and even sacrificing some of them. Who is to say that it won't be one of us next?"

Camille paused and Jeremy added his own thoughts. "Dude, we don't know who is going to be next but if it were you I would help you."

"Really?" Chase asked. "Why?"

"I don't know, just because," Jeremy replied. "If you want to get stronger with your gifts we can help you with that too."

Tyson sensed Chase's anger weakening and toned down his vampire appearance. Ethan kept his focus on Chase's thoughts.

"Yeah, I guess I would like that," Chase

shrugged. "I still am glad to be leaving here; I don't know how you live without computers and video games."

"I guess it is not for everybody," Nadine agreed. "It works for my family and personally I don't know how you live with all those distractions and chaos."

Tyson had now returned completely to his normal self and told Chase that they needed to talk privately before leaving. Chase agreed but requested that Mercy join them. They made their way back to the house, talking intently.

"Ok, I don't know about any of you; but that was crazy," Gretchen exclaimed. "He like went bonkers over nothing."

"Yeah, but Tyson was pretty sexy when he went all big and bad vampire on him," Zoe said, smiling an evil grin.

"Really, is that all you can think of is guys? I mean we have other issues like dying to think about too," Gretchen snapped.

"Remember, I am a Xana and that is what we do. I can't think of anything better to think of before I risk death," Zoe laughed.

Gretchen popped out of sight, not wanting Zoe to see she still had a bit of a crush on Tyson.

"Isn't anyone a little curious to where we are going next?" Ethan asked. "All I know is it is north of here and it is probably going to be secluded too."

"I think you may visit the mountain dwellers in Virginia," Nadine suggested. "I know that they are secluded from most people like us."

"They have lived in the mountains all their lives," Viho explained. "They are clever and extremely greedy, I have heard. They mine crystals and gold from places that no human can survive."

"So is that what makes them so special?" Jeremy asked.

Viho looked at Nadine for support. "There are two clans, one is the Asrais clan and the other the Appalachian tribe people. I don't know much about the Asrais Clan but I do know that the tribe people are very strong and can swim in water without breathing. I have also heard that they get everywhere in the city through tunnels."

"Asrais' are small but fierce fairies that my Auntie Rhiannon has told us stories about," Chloe explained. "I have never met one and honestly I thought they were just a tale. They should be fairly easy to deal with as long as they stay out of the sun and you don't restrain them, as legend has it."

For the rest of the afternoon they played and trained. They chased each other to see who was the fastest, wrestled to see who was the strongest, and practiced their gifts to see who was the most experienced. Near seven o'clock they gathered for dinner where they ate and talked about their experiences at Nina and Taj's home.

"On behalf of all us," Camille started while glancing at Chase, "we would like to thank you for your kindness, generosity and lessons. You have an amazing family and a wonderful retreat. Thank you for your safe harbor." Camille sat down after bowing towards Nina and Taj.

"It was our pleasure my dear and we will miss you all," Nina replied. "I hope to see all of you again someday. Taj and I know that you will do us proud in seeking out this plague that has taken aim on our young people. I have been blessed to see my old friends again with their children. The thought that I will not see some ever again hurts my heart."

Ethan pondered those words as they cleared the table and said their goodbyes.

Camille had not mentioned a vision of loss. Perhaps death awaited nonetheless and Zoe had the right idea. He tried not to imagine the two kids they had tried to save and what his father had had to do to remove them as a threat.

CHAPTER TWENTY

NIGHT TERROR

The sun seemed to rise too quickly for the children in the motor coaches. They had fallen asleep as soon as their heads touched their pillows. A faint outline of trees along a mountain side could be seen from the windows of each coach. They could also see movement in the trees as the coach slowed alone a rough stretch of road.

"Dad, I think there is something out there following us," Jeremy warned.

Luis leaned over toward Atticus' window for a closer look.

"I would be more concerned if there wasn't anything or anybody following us up here," Luis replied. "Those are the harpies."

Jeremy remembered a bedtime story that his mother would tell him. "If you go outside and see the trees bow with no wind on a summer day, hide in shadow for the things that come may be the harpies..."

"I thought that they were just a story Mom told us to get us to pay attention to everything around us," Jeremy replied.

Luis raised his left brow, as if to say 'you see, maybe we do know more than you.'

"So are they going to hurt us? Are they hunting us down?" Chase asked from his top bunk.

"Why are you so negative?" Tyson responded.

Chase rolled back under the covers, ignoring his step brother.

"I am not sure why they are whirling around so quickly," Atticus told Luis. "They are usually a little less obvious."

A minute later Atticus' phone rang. "What is going on here?" Atticus wondered.

He was certain he had turned his phone off after leaving the city.

"Hello," Atticus answered cautiously.

A frantic Helen was talking a mile a minute on the other end of the line.

"Slow down my love, I can't understand anything you are saying," Atticus said.

"We have been trying to contact you for nearly 30 minutes. I can't seem to connect to

Ethan and Senona was having trouble turning your phone on," Helen exclaimed. "There is some type of digital signal blocking our communication and leaving a trail of bread crumbs behind us."

Atticus knew that the boys had just woken up and his phone and GPS were all off.

"It can't be from here," he said. "You had to turn on my phone and there is nothing else that is connected. Why are you so frantic?" he asked.

Atticus could hear Senona and Monique in the back ground telling the girls to stay calm as Anthony maneuvered the motor coach down the steep mountain road.

"We are being rammed by a big rig, and something is knocking boulders onto the road that Anthony has to steer around," Helen explained. "Gabriel did come on board to see why we were so anxious. He sent some harpies to warn you to leave the road to the Asrais Clan and Appalachian tribesmen."

Atticus was only a mile from the exit to their hosts' private road; he had already started to slow the coach down to exit the mountain highway. Atticus told the boys to sit down and hold on as he changed gears and lanes to keep them moving. On speaker phone,

Atticus asked Anthony what he needed from them since they were a few miles ahead clearing the way.

"I need you figure out a way to get in behind me and deal with this big rig," Anthony exclaimed. "Senona has summoned ravens and crows to deal with the annoying rock thrower."

Atticus could hear the anger and fear in Anthony's voice, knowing that it took a lot of focus to guide a motor coach along the mountain side without having additional obstacles.

"You stay focused on keeping your cargo safe back there and we will figure a way back without notice," Atticus reassured him.

"10-4 my friend," Anthony replied, a bit out of character.

Helen took them off speaker phone and spoke with Atticus directly. "Gabriel told us that there is something on our coach or yours that is creating a digital pulse. It is more than likely that these are the mirror men attacking us. I would be lying if I said I wasn't scared a little," Helen added.

"I know my love, I am not going to lose you any sooner than nature says," Atticus reassured her. "I am going to take care of my end, but I am going to have to toss this phone and I recommend you do the same."

"I love you dear," Helen told her husband. "Tell Ethan I love him too. I am going to pass the phone to Senona who wants to speak with Luis for a minute, alright?"

"You there, sweetheart?" Luis asked.

"I am here you big sexy man," Senona replied. "I love you like crazy baby!"

"Ditto baby, ditto," Luis whispered with a soft Spanish accent, then hung up.

Luis handed the phone back to Atticus who immediately flung it down the side of the mountain. He geared down the coach and left the mountain road up an off ramp. As the coach rolled slowly to a stop, Atticus told the boys what he had just learned. Luis jumped out of the coach with Ethan to see if there was anything giving off a signal attached to the sides. He asked Tyson to check the inside of the coach, including the boys' luggage, to ensure that nothing had been hidden in them while they were at their last stop.

"All clear out here," Luis exclaimed as he and Ethan stepped back onto the coach.

Tyson reported that he had a faint tingle in his ear at the back of the coach.

"Ethan, come back here with me," Tyson said. "Do you hear that?"

Listening carefully, he thought he could detect a digital signal coming from the bunks.

"Up there, it is coming from up there," Ethan told Tyson.

'Up there' was Chase's bunk. Chase was buried under the covers, oblivious to what was going on.

Tyson yanked back the covers and found Chase playing a video game on his phone with his ear buds on.

"What is your problem?" Chase cried indignantly as Tyson ripped the phone and ear buds from him.

"Don't you move, or it will be the last time you move on your own," Tyson growled. "Jeremy, I need you to stand here and watch him as I bring these to your father."

"My pleasure." Jeremy postured himself in a guardian position.

Chase, who had been unaware of any issues, knew now that something was seriously wrong and that he was part of the problem.

"Bring him here quickly," Luis instructed Jeremy.

Chase jumped down from the bed as Jeremy all but carried him the 30 feet to the driver's area.

"Where did you get this phone and when?" Atticus demanded. He was now in full vampire form and was going to stop at nothing to save his wife and friends.

Hesitating in terror, Chase replied, "Sir, sir, I'm sorry. I took it from those kids' clothes. I didn't, didn't think they would need, need them. I just wanted to play a game. I didn't use the phone, I swear!"

"You said them," Atticus repeated slowly. "What did you mean by 'them'?"

Chase knew that he had to tell the truth; the consequences were unthinkable.

"Ah, ah, ah," Chase couldn't speak he was scared to death.

Ethan turned and placed his hand on Chase's head.

"There was an iPod or something that he took, too. He gave it to Zoe to shut her up, after she caught him with them," Ethan explained.

"You have threatened all of our safety," Atticus told Chase ominously.

"My Lord, I will deal with my step brother, I am truly sorry," Tyson intervened.

Atticus collected his thoughts and returned to his more human state.

"Yes, you will be dealing with him later. For now take him to his bunk and put him to sleep while you guard him," Atticus replied.

Handing the phone to Luis, who crushed it effortlessly in his hand, Atticus told everyone to sit down and hold on. He got the coach moving again over a bridge that crossed the highway where Anthony would be in less than 10 minutes.

"We are going to double back on the south bound side. I saw a median crossing three miles back where we will cut in behind the big rig. My friend, we are going to have to improvise from there," Atticus told Luis.

"Improvise is my middle name," Luis replied as he thought through possible options.

"My dad's got this one. He has to improvise all the time when renovating old houses to bring them up to code or meet LEED standards," Jeremy whispered to Ethan.

"I have no doubt that he will make something happen," Ethan whispered back.

They made it to the median cross over only moments before they could see Anthony driving toward them. Atticus had all the coach's lights off, with the diesel engine raring to go the minute the big rig passed them.

First Anthony passed, slowing as he noticed the motor coach in the median. The big rig then passed by, not slowing a bit. Atticus eased his coach out of the median, careful not to flip it, and then it was on. The diesel roared, the transmission screamed as the coach found power buried in 3rd gear, then 4th gear, then 5th gear. Atticus pulled his coach up as close to the big rig as he could.

Amazed that the driver hadn't noticed them, Atticus looked over at Luis. "Are you thinking what I am?"

"I think I am my friend," Luis replied. He started by easily opening the coach door against the rushing wind, followed by flinging himself up on top of the coach. Atticus instructed Jeremy to close the door to prevent any additional drag.

"Did you see my dad?" Jeremy asked aloud. "He just threw himself up there, where I am sure he is doing the old garg thing right now."

Jeremy was right. Without hesitation, Luis lunged onto the big rig in front of them with seemingly little effort.

"Sure glad that big guy is on our side," Atticus told the boys.

They watched as Luis made his way over the top of the rig toward the cab. Atticus stayed a safe distance behind, unsure exactly of Luis' plan.

When Luis reached the cab he carefully kneeled and lowered his head into the cab on the drivers' side. He saw the driver as expected, but was unprepared for a child in the passenger's seat. He had thought to yank or push the driver out from behind the wheel and take control of the rig. A child in the passenger seat complicated things.

As he was about to make his move, the child screamed, "Monster! Monster on the roof!"

The driver hit the air brakes, trying to sling Luis from the top of the rig. Luis had anticipated the move and secured himself for the quick movement of the big rig. Atticus had thought the scenarios through and had backed off some.

Luis leaned over on the passenger's side this time as he tried to gain control of the rig as it sped towards the other coach. The child once again screamed out in terror as Luis tried to enter the rig. This time he tried to reason with the driver, who sped along unconcerned for the safety of his own child.

"Please, allow me to help you with your rig," Luis offered, hanging through the window.

The driver looked over at the child and then back to the road with no intention of slowing down. Luis looked closely at the child who was still screaming but had nothing at all in his eyes.

"I know what you are doing here," Luis insisted. "I will get control of this vehicle."

The child closed her mouth, tilted her head towards him and then laughed. She answered, "I doubt it very much, you big freak."

The driver once again tried unsuccessfully to jerk Luis off the side of the truck. The child smiled and watched the road as they approached the other motor coach. Out of options, Luis knew he had no choice but to send the rig off the side of the mountain. He wasn't sure what the truck was towing in the container, though. If he could release the trailer he would feel a little better about sending just the cab off the mountain side. Luis swung out of the window, released the hose couplings to the cab and then unlocked the trailer that the container sat on. He had only seconds to get back to the cab and deliver a knockout blow to the head of the driver. Another leap to the driver's side and a swing of his massive gargoyle fist did the job. The driver's body slumped over the child; Luis grabbed hold of the steering wheel of the out of control big rig and cranked it around until the cab was heading into the guard rail. The 5 inch steel rail was no competition for this massive beast of steel. 'Thump, grind, thump grind.'

"What have you done?" the child screamed. "Help me! I am pinned under this guy."

Luis reminded himself that the child was only saying whatever she was told to fulfill the mirror men's plan.

'Thump, crack.' The rig broke through the railing and the trailer fell off the back end, rolling into the median. Luis stared at the driver and child then threw himself from the cab as it started to flip.

Atticus and the boys had been following Luis and the big rig from a safe distance.

"Where did my dad go?" Jeremy cried as the rig went over the guard rail.

Atticus slowed down the coach as they approached the last place they had seen Luis.

Applying the brakes and securing the coach, he told Tyson to not take his eyes off of Chase and for the other boys to stay inside until he knew it was safe.

Atticus stepped out of the coach and walked toward the edge of the cliff side. As he looked down he saw the smoke and flames bellowing up from the truck cab. He then had the feeling that someone was staring at him. He turned around to find his good friend leaning against the back side of the coach.

"You cut that a little close didn't you?" Atticus said dryly.

"You know how it these days; everyone wants a little extra drama with their action," Luis replied.

"Was there a child driving the big rig?" Atticus asked.

Luis chuckled. "No, but there was a child in the passenger seat and I guess you know what kind of child too."

As Atticus replied "Mirror men," Ethan threw open the door of the coach.

"We still have an issue," he exclaimed. "Mom just contacted me and said that something was still plummeting rocks at them."

Atticus jumped into coach followed by Luis. The roar of the diesel engine echoed along the sheer mountain face when he stomped on the pedal.

"How far ahead do you think they are?" Ethan asked.

Tyson and Atticus replied in unison, "Four miles."

A vampire trait that Ethan had not developed yet was the use of 'pinging'.

"I can't wait till I can ping," Ethan said.

Luis moved to the seating area of the coach where Jeremy was seated quietly.

"What's the matter big guy?" Luis asked his son, wrapping his arm over his shoulder.

Jeremy leaned into his dad's body and replied, "When I saw you go over the side with the truck, well I thought that maybe, you know?"

Luis wasn't good with expressing those feelings either. "I don't know when my day will come but you know if it were today you and Max would have seen me fighting for your future and that would have made me happy."

Jeremy replied, "Well you did look awesome jumping onto the truck and saving us."

Max ran up from the back where he was keeping an eye on Chase with Tyson and jumped into his dad's lap.

"There they are," Atticus announced,

"stopped along the side of the highway, but I don't sense a threat."

Once the coach came to a stop behind the others, Atticus and Luis jumped out. Helen, Senona, Monique and Anthony were standing in front of their coach looking into the dawn sky.

"Is everyone alright?" Atticus asked. "Why are you looking up in the sky?"

Embracing her husband, Helen replied, "Wait for it!"

The children had all left the coaches, with the exception of Tyson and Chase. They gathered beside their parents and looked up.

"Wow," Helen sighed.

"Beautiful," Camille exclaimed.

"Gorgeous, simply amazing," Senona added.

The children stood with their mouths open as a luminescent winged creature glided towards them in a circular pattern. The creature became larger and more mesmerizing as it approached. Even the wind of the harpies that buffeted them was not enough to distract their gaze. The amazing creature gently pulled in its 40 foot wing span and landed in the median.

"Quickly, get a blanket for her," Senona asked the girls.

"Her?" Jeremy said aloud.

Camille smiled and replied, "Yes, her. That gorgeous powerful creature is..."

"Jia!" Max shouted out with excitement.

"No way," Jeremy replied, in shock.

"Yes way," Chloe and Zoe affirmed.

Jia had shifted back to her human form by now and Gretchen had covered her with a quilt. Luis picked her up and brought her to their side of the road.

"I am so sorry that I no have the creature that throw rocks at us," Jia said with sorrow. "I pick up girl on horse that kick rocks but when I get to fly the girl tell horse to kick at me."

Lowering her head she explained, "Kicking hurt! I drop them from very high in the air into trees where could not go."

"It is alright my dear," Helen assured her. "What you did to help us was very honorable."

The children circled Jia thanking her and telling her how magnificent her dragon was.

"Looks like you two could probably use a rest," Atticus said smiling at Luis and Jia. "However it is probably not safe to take the planned route to the Appalachians' tunnels.

I am not familiar enough with this area to know any other entrance."

Senona and Monique collected the children back onto the coach, where Luis placed Jia on a chair.

Senona gave Luis a hug. "You never stop amazing me, you handsome, sexy creature."

Jeremy rolled his eyes as Max gave an approving smile.

"I am so confused with my mythology," Jeremy complained. "I thought that Asian dragons didn't fly or have wings."

Softly Jia replied, "It is the mythology scholars that are confused. They try too hard to make sense of dragons, with no regards for nature improvements."

"I think it's cool that something as small and delicate as you can be so big and dangerous," Zoe added with a hint of envy.

Anthony interrupted. "It's great that we're all safe and the harpies are doing their thing to protect the area. But traffic is going to pick up soon and we need someplace safe to go."

"We still don't know how they tracked us down," Monique added.

"Wrong," Atticus said. "That we do know, and we need Zoe out here before we go anywhere else."

Confused by Atticus' tone of voice, Monique entered the coach and told Zoe that they needed her outside.

"Cool, Mom, but what is the urgency?" Zoe replied. "I am learning more about Jia right now."

Monique wasn't in the mood for teenage back talk. She stared directly into Zoe's spirit with her fairy summoning gaze. Zoe jumped up, crying out for her to stop while she made her way off the coach.

Helen knew that Zoe had been trying her mother and father's patience and decided to deal with this issue herself. Holding Zoe's hand, Helen told her that Chase had admitted to taking a phone and iPod from those kids.

"We need the iPod that he gave you," Helen explained. "It is how these things are tracking us."

Monique shook her head. "What iPod? When did you get an iPod?"

"Mom, I didn't do it, I don't have... I don't...," Zoe couldn't lie while Helen was holding her hand.

"Zoe, we just want the iPod. We will deal with the rest later," Helen said firmly.

Zoe reached into her jeans and pulled out

the iPod while explaining that she just wanted to listen to some tunes in the coach.

Handing the device the Luis to crush, Helen let go of Zoe's hand while Monique grabbed it.

"Now that one issue has been addressed I suppose it is time for you to get out of here before this becomes a crime scene and no one goes anywhere," Gabriel said as he popped in out of nowhere once again.

Frustrated, Anthony explained to Gabriel that they had a bit of a problem.

"We can't go back and we don't know how to get there from here," Anthony elaborated.

"You see that ramp ahead of us? That is called a runaway ramp, only used if a big rig loses its brakes or has an emergency," Gabriel explained. "I want you to drive down this hill then cut off onto the runaway ramp and drive into the side of the mountain, where you will see me standing."

"Run into the side of the mountain," Anthony laughed. "Is there a time warp there too?"

Gabriel placed his hand on Anthony's shoulder and told him to take another big breath. Anthony sighed as his anxiety dissipated.

"The harpies and I will be waiting there for you. Trust me; there is a secret opening that our Appalachian friends use for emergencies. It is big enough to get both your coaches in. Then make a hard turn to the left where you will find an old mining track you can follow to its end," Gabriel continued.

Anthony and Atticus started the coaches up, released the air brakes and started down the incline of the mountain with their eyes fixed on the runaway ramp. Anthony hit the ramp hard shaking everyone and everything on the coach.

"Hold on!" he shouted as he changed gears. He drove up the rough ramp into what appeared to be trees and solid stone. He saw Gabriel standing directly in front of him and the harpies circling from side to side of a 15 foot area.

Taking a deep breath, he did as he was instructed. They roared into Gabriel and the solid mountain face with Atticus following close behind.

They were now inside the mountain. Some kind of illusion had made it appear solid, but they had passed through unscathed.

The bright lights of the coaches illuminated the pitch black inside the mountain. They turned hard to the left where they saw the large mining shaft that Gabriel had spoken of. Neither driver stopped once they were inside. An hour later they reached the end of the track and a crossroad. Unsure of where to go, they decided to await further instructions. The children went back to sleep while the adults discussed the events of the night. Consequences would face Chase and Zoe, the severity of which was a subject of much debate.

CHAPTER TWENTY ONE

NOT WANTED

'Thump, Thump' reverberated on the door of the coach.

"Who's there?" Luis asked. A large-framed person's silhouette shadowed the entrance.

"You sure made things more difficult than necessary on your way here," a deep voice replied.

"Wasn't exactly what we planned either, I can assure you," Luis stated. "We were all ready to get here early enough to roast some wieners and make s'mores with you before going to bed."

The deep-voiced man laughed. "You always did have a way of getting us to loosen up and have fun."

He cleared his throat and bellowed, "Open the shroud!"

Within seconds the entire cave and tunnel lit up with diffused light.

"You would have done better to keep that big mouth of yours closed, Julian," Luis told their host.

"No one calls me by that name," Julian said darkly.

"No one besides me, Julian," Luis repeated.

Julian knew snorted at his old friend's banter. They embraced in a test of strength, measuring which one would tap out first.

"We knew nothing of the earlier occurrence," Luis confirmed. "Please accept my deepest apologies for any possible threat that may have arisen."

Julian shrugged. "We always have some kind of excitement going on. Why should it be any different today? I should tell you that he is not very pleased about your staying here and is petitioning the elders to have you leave as soon as possible."

"We weren't expecting open arms. However, we are here at the elders' request, in search of that which threatens us all," Luis responded loudly, knowing that Nico, Julian's chief, was not far off.

Julian winked at Luis in a silent reassurance that Nico had heard him.

"So where are the families?" Julian asked.

"I suppose I could ask you the same thing," Luis replied. He nodded toward the coach and everyone started to file out.

"I know it has been a while, but I am sure you remember mi bella esposa Senona and these are my boys Jeremy and Max," Luis said as Julian kissed Senona's hand.

"Boys, this is my old friend Bear," Luis said with a smile.

"He doesn't look like a bear," Max commented. "That is a strange name for a man."

"That is his undercover name because too many people knew him by his other name," Luis explained. Truthfully, Julian had never been fond of his given name and took his totem animal as an alias.

"You are hairy and really big like a bear, so I think you are a bear," Max decided.

A few giggles rang from the nooks in the cave and even Julian gave a chuckle.

Luis finished the introductions, including everyone except Atticus and his family. Atticus stepped down from the coach last and lifted his hand. "My friend, I am grateful to have safe shelter with your tribe as the elders have prescribed. If my presence causes discomfort, I will plead with the elders to remove me. Please allow our children to stay so they can fulfill the prophecy."

Julian took a deep breath before replying, "You always did have a lot to say, my Lord. Even if some here do not wish to receive you, the elders have spoken and you are our guest. Nico has sent his family to stay in other areas of our caverns, and others have chosen to have no contact with you or your families. I hope that your stay is not too long but as deputy will furnish whatever you need for your mission."

"Fair enough old friend," Atticus acknowledged, and shook Julian's hand as a sign of peace.

"Allow me to introduce my wife Helen and my son Ethan," Atticus said.

"Pleasure to make your acquaintance Mr. Bear," Ethan said as he shook Julian's hand.

"Smart boy you got there," Julian replied winking at Atticus. "Let me fetch mine now."

Julian yelled for his family to make their way down to meet their guests. Three young boys jumped out of the ceiling of the cavern while a young stocky woman walked towards them.

"This is my bride Aurora," Julian introduced.

"It is nice to meet all of you," Aurora greeted them. "We don't have a lot of visitors, as you can imagine."

"On my right here is our oldest son Talon," Julian continued, "and this is our daughter Ivy. Don't let how tidy she looks fool you; she can get dirtier than all the boys if she wants something. These are our twins Colt and this bouncy one is Digger, if it is not bolted down he thinks it belongs to him."

They all looked a little rough around the edges, but were dressed well for living in caves and tunnels. Aurora and Ivy even looked like they could do some fashion modeling for an outdoor magazine.

"It is our pleasure to meet everyone finally," Helen said. "I have heard some tales about my husband's time here and they are quite something. He explained that you share your community with the Grottoasrais and their Queen Jasmine."

"I am sure he has told some stories about them," Julian replied with a deep laugh. "Yes, we all have amicable living arrangements with Jasmine and her family. Unfortunately you will have to wait until later to meet them. They don't care much for the daylight." Julian added, "I am sure Atticus has explained why."

"Are the Grottaserais fairy vampires? I thought they were fairies but if they don't like daylight, then maybe they are vampires, too," Max speculated.

"No, they are definitely not vampires," Ivy stated defensively.

"Why don't you let my children show yours around? We need to figure out what to do with these loud beasts you arrived in," Julian instructed.

"Sounds like a plan to me," Luis agreed. "Maybe you and I could sit down with Nico and some of that good honey juice that we used to drink?"

The children didn't wait for additional instructions. Ivy grabbed hold of Ethan's hand and ran down one of the tunnels at the crossroad. The others followed in hot pursuit, curiosity and protectiveness vying for predominance.

"Wait up," Gretchen yelled out to Ivy and Ethan.

Ivy looked at Ethan. "If anyone should be able to keep up, you would think it would be her."

Jeremy was holding Max's hand at the back of the group, jogging to keep Ethan in sight.

"Camille, do you know where she is taking us?" Jeremy called out.

Camille had a brief picture of where they were going and quickly reassured Jeremy.

A faint light spilled into the cavern in front of them. Ethan hoped it was where they were going because he was getting tired.

As the light grew closer, the temperature change suggested that they were getting closer to the outside of the cavern. In less than a minute they broke through some brush and were outside in the early morning air.

"Why were we running so fast just to get outside?" Ethan asked as he tried to catch his breath.

"It is easier to talk out here than in there," Talon explained.

Ethan, Gretchen, Camille, Jeremy, Max, Talon, Colt, Digger, Chloe, Jia and Ivy were standing on the side of the mountain face. A 200 foot drop fell to one side, the cavern shadowed the other and before them the sun shone over a forested valley.

"We were told that there were nine kids with you. Where are the other two?" Talon asked.

Jeremy looked hesitantly at his companions, and then explained to his new friends that Zoe and Chase were under a type of docile spell cast by his mother. "They have to stay still and not speak unless spoken to."

"I would die if I couldn't talk," Ivy declared.

"Wouldn't that be a dream come true," Colt exclaimed.

Ivy gave him disgusted look. She explained to the others that it was easier to talk in the daylight because the caverns talked; there were no secrets in a cavern.

They hiked away from the cave entrance and soon located a large freshwater spring coursing between two mountain peaks, with only blue sky above them. Ethan paused and stared for a moment. He recognized this place from a dream and had drawn a picture of it in his diary. Something was significant about this place but he couldn't put his finger on it.

"It's safe here," Ivy said. "Let's talk about those mirror men things."

Talon continued, "We have heard plenty of stories of how these things can take over your body and mind and make you do anything. Why do you think they are targeting kids like us? Is it forever if they do turn us, and why do you call them mirror men instead of zombie kids or droids?"

"I will try to answer your questions the best I can," Camille answered, assuming her role as the spokesman of their group. "First, we call them mirror men because originally when we encountered them their eyes were vacant and reflected back only what they saw, like a mirror. But the ones we encountered this past week in North Carolina were different. They seemed more normal in their speech and movements, but their eyes still did not focus properly. That tells us that they are evolving to avoid recognition.

"We first encountered them at our families' Beltane festival three years ago," Camille explained. "At first we were not sure what or who they were. I thought that they were rogue kids who wanted to start trouble; however, when they tried to kill us we quickly understood there was more going on."

"Yeah, but you should have seen Ethan's and my dad take that mirror man down," Jeremy exclaimed.

"I am sure that they had very little trouble," Talon replied. "We have heard plenty of stories about Luis Santiago of Valencia and Lord Atticus, the last Noble King to the vampires."

Jeremy looked at Ethan oddly, previously unaware of his father's fame.

"They seem to only interact with kids," Camille continued. "They are very suspicious of adults and even though they have attacked many of our kind around the world they do infect quotidian children, too. The elders have set up micro-cells of gifted and quotidian children around the world to infiltrate the mirror men and find out whom or what is controlling them. Anywhere we have any interaction with them we leave a sign."

Camille turned to Max to ask him to draw the COTO brush stroke symbol. Ivy piped in, "Does it look like this?" She took a stone and carefully started drawing a COTO symbol.

"Yes, that is it," Max agreed in surprise, "but how did you know?"

"We were in the Serenity Channel when we saw one the first time," Ivy said. "We heard a few years back someone decided to use this symbol or an ankh to tag the mirror men."

"Camille was the one that thought of that idea," Gretchen interjected. "We track the locations on a map in the Serenity Channel and also with an app that Simon designed for smart phones," Gretchen added.

"Have you had any contact with the mirror men?" Camille asked, hoping that her timing was right. She was interested in what Talon and his tribe had witnessed but knew that she needed their trust to get their information.

"A few encounters," Talon said. "We can reach the city in minutes through our tunnels. A few of them have tried to follow us back through the tunnels. They don't get very far before they turn around and head back to the surface. Once, this kid just about grabbed my jacket then just stopped and turned around. Weird, right?"

"Not really. We think that they need an energy source to connect to one another as well as to stay coherent," Camille explained. "I can't imagine that it is very easy to get a radio or satellite signal in your tunnels and caves."

Ivy and the others laughed. "No it is not easy at all. This makes Chief Nico very frustrated when he is playing his lottery games. He has to go to the top of the north tower cavern and almost stick his head out," Ivy said.

"He must be careful. We now know that they can track signals when they have your phone number or device status," Chloe warned. "My sister almost got us killed because she was listening to music on a stupid iPod that she got from Chase, who stole it from a mirror man!"

An uncomfortable silence fell on the group. Camille sensed the change and asked, "So, what do you guys do for fun in place of television and on-line stuff?"

"Follow me," Digger offered. "I'll show you some real fun."

Jeremy, Ethan and Max didn't have to be told twice. They followed Digger and Colt to a hole at the edge of the freshwater spring. Digger, then Colt climbed into the opening and then let go of the edge. They started down the side of the mountain on a natural water slide.

"Come on, scaredy cats," Jeremy shouted back to the girls and Talon. He raced after the other boys.

"It's the fastest and the easiest way down the mountain for everyone here," Ivy told the rest. "Everyone except Gretchen, I guess," Ivy added as she let go and slid down the water slide.

The spring shimmered slightly before Gretchen's eyes. She blinked once and for a moment the water was replaced by a meadow surrounded by oak trees. She took a step and the spring materialized again. Turning to look for Camille, Gretchen realized she was the last one left on top of the mountain. Shrugging, she hurled herself into the hole after the others.

CHAPTER TWENTY TWO

INDEPENDENCE DAY?

"It has been nice to have a few quiet days here with you and your family," Senona told Aurora and Jasmine.

Helen, Monique and Mercy agreed. Worrying over their children and the mirror men had prevented the relaxation normally associated with a vacation. Senona had been wearing her hands off writing articles with paper and pen. Mercy had to send them to the periodicals via snail mail since the use of computers and email was off limits.

Jasmine, queen of the Grottoasrais, sighed. "It has been a joy to have you all here. Too long have our families fought and felt the pain of lost love. My girls and Aurora's children are having an amazing time with yours. They now know one another and can trust each other. Unfortunately, Chief Nico has terrified many of the others regarding your stay and they have hidden their children deep within the caves of these mountains."

Senona and Helen knew that she was referring to what happened with Atticus, Nico, Jose and Victoria.

"It is sad that such long-ago events, horrific though they were, still hinder our families," Senona replied. "My husband and Lord Atticus are here for a much greater cause." Senona knew others were listening in hiding and wanted to announce their good intentions.

"I know, my dear; Julian, Aurora and I have tried to reason with Nico to no avail. I am but the queen of a small clan of Grottoasrais. We depend on the strength of the Appalachian tribe to give us safe shelter after our migration from the sea," Jasmine explained.

Nothing more needed to be said. Senona, Helen, Monique and Mercy knew how hard-headed the old clan chiefs could be. They agreed that their stay would be as short but productive as possible.

The next few days passed smoothly. Only once were Colt and Jeremy spotted while they were having a watermelon seed spitting contest over a busy roadway.

"Oops," Jeremy yelped. He dropped the piece of melon that they were eating and spitting seeds from. It landed on the hood of a passing car with a huge thump. The car wasn't damaged but the driver was startled and angry when he looked back and saw the two of them. Colt jumped from half-way down the sign pole with Jeremy not far behind. The driver of the car had pulled over and was in hot pursuit by foot.

"Follow me, I have a secret pathway," Colt yelled. "Run faster."

Jeremy thought if he could run faster he would. One of the tribe's gifts was the ability to manipulate the elements of earth and air. Right now, Colt was using the air to speed up his running. The driver was gaining ground on Jeremy. Colt jumped over the guard rail and disappeared into the earth, which had opened to conceal him.

Jeremy knew he wasn't going to make it. He jumped over the guard rail and chanted,

"Bushes, trees, butterflies and bees; earth give me cover please."

As Jeremy hit the ground, vines, bushes and shrub trees buried him, while butterflies and bees fluttered and swarmed along the guard rail.

"I don't know where you kids went but if I had caught you I was going to...," the angry driver yelled as the bees buzzed towards him.

The driver ran back to his car. Jeremy lay in the dirt for a few more minutes to avoid detection. Crawling out and brushing dirt off, he thanked the vegetation for their cover.

"That was pretty good," Colt said. He was only 20 feet away, half of his body in the ground.

"Thanks; it was better than getting caught and having to deal with my parents," Jeremy replied. "You weren't bad yourself. I knew you guys had moves but you were really fast. Sorry about the watermelon; I know you love watermelons," Jeremy added.

Earlier Colt had told Jeremy and the others about how excited he was with the early spring and how a local farmer had planted early this year. Colt spent several months chasing off rodents and animals from the farmer's field. Then he could help himself to a few extra melons in exchange for his services, unbeknownst to the farmer.

"Yeah that kind of sucked, but I have more back at my secret holding area," Colt replied as they headed back into the mountain along a lower path. On the way Colt explained how his brother Digger had helped break through some granite in the far part of the farmer's field so that they could watch the watermelons grow everyday without anyone seeing them.

"Jeremy, Jeremy we are going to a party tonight," Max shouted out as soon as he saw him. "There is going to be lots of food and really big star crackers and boomers!"

Colt looked at Jeremy, confused.

"Star crackers and boomers are Max's names for firecrackers and fireworks," Jeremy explained.

"That's right, today is the 4th of July!" Colt replied.

Ethan, Camille, Gretchen and Ivy weren't far behind Max. They explained that when they went to the store to pick up Whoppers for Chief Nico, they heard people talking about the big town party planned for tonight.

"Cool, we're going to a party," Jeremy said. "Wait a minute, this isn't some lame town with one flashing light that thinks safety first and uses Walmart fireworks, is it?"

Jeremy had read some books about the different states he would be traveling through. When he thought about the mountains of

Virginia and West Virginia, some backwoods stereotypes came to mind.

"Not at all," Julia replied.

Jeremy was tongue-tied when he saw Julia, which was quite unusual for him. All the Grottoasrais' were tiny and pretty, but there was just something about Julia that made Jeremy speechless. Julianna was very pretty and quiet, Jaden was spunky and Jenny was fun but trouble. Julia was smart and had a sophisticated demeanor to her, like a mix of Camille and Gretchen but without the sisterly nagging.

"Lexington Virginia is hosting the 4th of July celebration this year," Julia explained. "It is only 10 miles from here and it is a very culturally diverse and historical city of around 7000 people plus the student body."

Jeremy didn't understand what that had to do with being a good city for a 4th of July party, but it sounded good coming from Julia.

"What my sister is saying is that it is a great place for young people after dark, which is the only time we get out anyway," Jenny clarified. "The Virginia Military Academy and the historical Washington and Lee University are there, which means lots of hotties studying to be doctors, musicians, lawyers, engineers and neuroscientists."

Camille, Gretchen, Jia and Chloe raised their eyebrows, interested.

"Come on girls, Ivy and I can get you all looking fabulous," Julianna whispered. "I can make you look 21," she added.

Chloe replied, "You take care of them, I'm covered."

Jeremy looked at the other guys. "I guess we need a shower. Hey, what's up with the Whoppers for Chief Nico anyway?"

"He's just got a sweet tooth and he is always having one of us getting him Whoppers or Butterfingers," Talon laughed.

"I feel bad going to this 4th of July party in Lexington without the children," Helen fretted. "I have blocked Ethan all day to not let him know or worry him."

Aurora and Jasmine had decided to go into Lexington for the celebrations. "It will be good for us adults to have one night out with thousands of other people celebrating their independence," Aurora explained. "The children have been having so much fun in and around the mountain and tunnels that they won't even miss us."

"Aurora is right; the children have been teaching each other new skills and playing for several days straight. Last night they fell asleep somewhere in a cave after sharing ghost stories. I suppose a few hours away won't hurt anything," Helen admitted.

"It is getting late. I will let the Chief know that we will be leaving for a few hours and to have the children play or practice when they get back from their adventures," Jasmine said.

An hour later they were on their way to Lexington. Anthony and Atticus had already left to meet a few of the elders in a distant part of the cave system. Tyson and Mercy had met some new friends that didn't mind that they had to drag Zoe and Chase along with them.

"Luis, Avery, Julian, you guys think you can handle a few extra woman tonight?" Jasmine asked flirtatiously.

"Wow!" Julian said as he looked at the ladies.

"Wow, caliente!" Luis added. "I better watch that I don't get burned."

"I love you, you big hot sexy romantic lug," Senona giggled.

The guys put their arms out for their ladies

and they left for Lexington through a fairy channel.

"Are you sure this is alright with our parents?" Ethan asked Ivy when she came looking for them.

Ethan was uneasy. He wasn't able to connect with his mother and he knew that they hadn't had any contact with elders or mirror men in several days.

"Everything is cool. I talked with Chief Nico and he said that our parents were off doing some ritual and they wouldn't mind if we went to Lexington for a few hours to see the fireworks," Ivy assured him. "As a matter of fact, I think he is just happy that we are not bothering him."

"Am I ever going to meet Chief Nico? Is he even a real Chief?" Ethan asked as Julia and Jenny approached.

Ivy took a deep breath. "He is very real and my father is his deputy."

"I hope you don't ever meet him," Jenny added as she got closer. "There is bad blood between him and your father. Since you're in Lord Atticus' blood line, you are hated too."

"By him, not us," Julia added.

Ethan sighed, "OK, well I'll go tell the other guys that you are ready to go, alright?"

Julia nodded. "You did tell him that we were going, didn't you?" she asked Ivy.

"YES, of course I told him and he was really nice about it too," Ivy replied. "Even gave me some advice."

Ethan returned with the guys moments later. One by one the girls appeared from the shadows of the cave and adjoining tunnels, dressed to the extreme.

The guys' jaws dropped as Camille, Gretchen, Jia, and Chloe entered.

Swallowing hard, Jeremy said "I can't believe it is really you guys! You all look so much older and well..."

"What Jeremy is trying to say is that you all are very beautiful and we are proud to accompany you to the 4th of July celebration," Ethan explained.

Ethan had learned his gentleman skills from watching his father.

"That was pretty close to what I meant, but you look really hot too!" Jeremy added.

Chloe, Jenny, Jaden, Julianna and Julia smiled and batted their eyes at Jeremy. Camille, Gretchen and Jia were not as comfortable with being called hot.

"We better go if we want to get there before they ignite the fireworks," Talon urged.

"We have to get there before the spark crackers and boomers," Max repeated excitedly.

"It takes us a little longer than the older Grottoasrais and Appalachians because we don't have those gifts yet," Talon explained.

"Yeah, but we have a short cut," Digger added.

"As long as it doesn't include a water slide down the side of the mountain," Chloe replied. "My hair was a mess for two days!"

Talon snorted and led them to a far tunnel. In less than an hour they heard music and laughter outside of the solid walls.

"You are going to love this," Jenny said.

Talon pushed on the stone where a dim light shone through.

"Give me a hand garg boy," Talon asked Jeremy as they pushed on the wall.

The wall opened into an office, not any office but the President of Education's office.

"That explains why the door was stiff," Talon said. The book case door that was installed and forgotten about in the late 1700's had a chair up propped against it.

"I guess the President is remodeling the office," Colt observed.

"Aren't you afraid of getting caught coming through the boss' office?" Gretchen asked.

They all laughed. "He is rarely in his office for starters, but if he were here we would slip back out and come in another secret passage. The contractors built several into the original building so they could come back and steal what was rightfully theirs if they didn't get paid in full," Julia explained. "There's supposed to be a tunnel that goes from here to Washington D.C. Someday Talon or Julian will find it."

"Yeah but what if you got caught in the room?" Ethan persisted.

"You guys worry too much," Jaden said. "Everyone knows that ghosts haunt this place. Robert E. Lee still shouts out military orders from his grave here in Lexington. So we would just pretend we are ghosts!" Jaden glanced at Gretchen.

"Enough with the history lesson," Jenny and Chloe said in unison. "Let's go find some college boys and see some fireworks."

Walking onto the college campus through the massive colonnade, Camille could imagine herself there one day. She stared up at the massive statue of George Washington standing high above the school.

"I hope someday we can be in an open and tolerant environment like this college," Camille said wistfully. "However, I think that even in another 200 years we will still just be leaving shadows like now."

"I agree," Julia replied. "Although technically I can't leave real shadows, but tonight we will leave shadows in the light of fireworks with new friends." Julia grabbed Camille's hand and ran down the lawn towards the others.

They left the school property and headed into town. The town was packed with people dressed in celebratory clothing, waving flags and eating. Ivy had brought a purse of money that she had collected. "Here, each of you can have $10.00 to buy anything you want," she offered. "I am going over there with the turkey legs and corn dogs."

"Corn dogs! Please Jeremy can I have a corn dog?" Max asked.

"I don't see why not. We are permitted to eat corn and I am not sure what is in a wiener, but I suppose one corn dog isn't going to hurt," Jeremy reasoned.

"Forget the food," Chloe suggested, checking out the guys.

"We have to have a plan," Julia decided. "Talon, Jeremy, Max, Colt will stay with my sisters, Jia and Chloe. Ethan and Digger will stay with Camille, Gretchen, Ivy and me. This way we have someone who knows their way around and we can use our gifts to communicate if needed."

"Fine, are you done with the hand holding now, MOM?" Jenny complained. "We know, stay together, stay out of trouble and watch our backs."

"One more thing," Camille added. "Enjoy yourselves and we will meet back here a half hour after the fireworks are over."

Everyone agreed and headed out into the crowd.

Lexington was busy and no one was paying them much attention. Plenty of students were milling around even though school was technically out for summer. Families spread out on picnic blankets and lawn chairs. The music they had heard earlier was now 10 times louder and the crowd was waiting for the fireworks, which were delayed due to some technical difficulty.

Talon and Jeremy weren't enjoying themselves quite as much as they could have because they had to keep the boys and men off of Jenny, Julianna, Chloe and Jaden. The girls were enjoying the attention and Max was getting loved on by the girls.

"Is it always like this when they go out?" Jeremy asked Talon and Colt.

"Pretty much, I guess their gift of love is both a blessing and a curse, at least until sunrise." Talon replied. "Julianna likes the attention but doesn't like being touched so she will be the first one we will have to assist."

Julia stayed just far enough away from her sisters to still be able to see them. Camille, Gretchen and Ethan could see that Julia was preoccupied so they talked with Digger and Ivy about the people they saw and the music.

"I like the patriotic music but you think they could play current stuff, too," Gretchen said. "Some Lady Gaga, Katy Perry or even some Aerosmith would be a nice change."

"I love all those artists and do you know Luke Bryan, Taylor Swift and Band Perry?" Ivy asked "I love them too!"

Gretchen agreed that they were all great and that Luke Bryan was from near where they lived.

Camille stopped suddenly. Gretchen

instructed Julia to stand on one side of Camille.

"What's happening? Is she OK? Did she eat something she shouldn't have?" Ivy asked.

Gretchen explained that she was having a vision. The first firework shot into the air and exploded. Camille's body shook violently. Digger and Ethan held her steady and Gretchen assured her everything was alright.

"Camille, Ethan, Gretchen!" Chloe screamed from the other side of a huge crowd. "They're here, they're here!" she yelled.

Gretchen only heard Camille's name but she felt the energy of the scream and she knew it was not positive. The second firework exploded in the air raining down a shower of red, white and blue stars as Camille shook and opened her eyes.

"They're here, and they knew we were here, but I don't know how," Camille said frantically.

"Who is here?" Digger asked.

"The mirror men, and lots of them too," Camille said. "I think our parents are here as well; I saw them in my vision. We need to get the others and figure a way back to the tunnels."

"They're over there. Chloe is shouting

something so she must have seen them too," Gretchen said.

Camille concentrated on Chloe but couldn't connect. "Ethan I need you to..."

Ethan knew what he had to do. He concentrated on Chloe and asked her what she saw and how to get out of there.

"Chloe says that she saw the same kids from the park in North Carolina. They were all over the place. She doesn't think that they have seen them yet or made the connection," Ethan explained.

"Tell her to try to make it to the colonnade. We'll meet them if we can," Camille instructed Ethan. A series of fireworks went off over their heads in a massive light show.

Ethan forwarded the message to Chloe.

"I am picking up something else," Ethan told Camille. "It's my mother and she is here with Julia's mother and Ivy's parents, Jeremy's parents and Chloe's parents."

"Ethan where are you?" Helen cried inside his head.

"We are over here," Ethan replied as he tried to project an image of a display selling LED hats, flags and necklaces. "Jeremy, Max, Chloe, Jaden, Julianna, Jenny, Jia, Talon and Colt are on the other side near the stage."

Ethan shared this information with Chloe so she could keep an eye out for them.

The fireworks kept lighting up the sky as they tried to work their way out of the crowd.

"Please don't touch me, let go, let go please," Julianna exclaimed as she reached her limit.

They had been made by the mirror men. So many people clustered around Jeremy, Talon and Colt that they couldn't really help Julianna. Talon grabbed Jenny's hand, Jeremy grabbed Max's hand and they ran through the crowd. They tried to keep an eye on Julia. They knew that they had to stay separated to avoid capture.

"Maybe Max can draw us out of here," Jeremy thought aloud.

"With what and where?" Chloe asked. "He doesn't have anything to make a picture with and besides, they would follow."

"There's my mother and your parents and Jeremy's parents too," Ethan told the others when he saw them finally.

Luis kept them moving to the back of the crowd. He explained that the mirror men weren't going to do anything if they were going to be caught. Apparently they had not yet detected Ethan and Camille's group, so they kept moving back, hoping to slip away.

Once they reached the back of the crowd, a fine smoke started to cover the ground. The fireworks still created an awesome visual spectacle in the sky, holding the crowd's attention. Ethan could see that the mirror men had circled around Jeremy and the others. He also saw Luis, Julian and Avery working on some plan.

"Ethan, Luis is going to create a distraction by taking down one of the mirror men. There is another tunnel only a hundred yards away," Helen told him. "You need to head for that tunnel and we will follow behind and lose them."

"I don't know what your mother is saying to you, Ethan, but it is too late. They see us now," Camille told Ethan.

Like a magnet all the mirror men began swarming towards Ethan, leaving the other group free to go.

"What just happened?" Julian bellowed.

"Go Mother, we can get out of here! The Jinn can get us out; you leave while you have the chance," Julia cried.

Luis held Jeremy back as he struggled to follow the mirror men, intent on attacking them. Monique and Jasmine opened a port and left. Talon collected the sisters and herded them towards the adults.

"She is right, we need to go now," Senona insisted. "There is more to this situation. We need to figure it out so we can help."

"Jinn, you need to get us out of here now," Julia and Ivy said urgently.

The mirror men were only 40 yards away and moving slowly but still getting closer.

"Now Jinn, now!" Ivy cried.

"Who are Jinn and where are they?" Ethan asked.

Camille had seen it and now the vision made sense. "Gretchen, you are the Jinn. You need to get us out of here now."

Camille grabbed a nearby blanket and laid it quickly on the ground.

"Everyone step onto the blanket. We need to stay attached to this blanket or we will be lost in time," Camille explained hurriedly.

"I still don't understand," Gretchen cried. "I am not a Jinn. I am nothing but a ghost girl."

"No, you are a Jinn. I saw it and the DM's see it too. You need to focus on getting us out of here. Focus on anywhere but here right now," Camille exhorted. "Try Gretchen, please try!"

Ethan crept into Gretchen's mind to calm her. Julia held her hand. The crowd shimmered and like nothing had ever happened they were gone from the 4th of July celebration in Lexington Virginia. The mirror men threat was gone, but they didn't know where they were.

"Thank you, thank you Gretchen," Camille and Julia cried, hugging her while staying on the blanket.

"Now that I have seen how crazy those mirror men really are, I am going to keep close to my brothers," Ivy exclaimed. "I have never been so scared in my life."

Ethan and Digger didn't say anything. They were still trying to catch their breath after being prepared to fight.

"I didn't know I was a Jinn or Genie. How could I not know that? Why would my dad not tell me this? How did you know?" Gretchen asked Ivy and Julia.

"The Appalachian tribes people were cursed long ago with a witch's spell. We see everyone for their true self," Ivy explained. "One of the reasons that we cohabitate so well with the Grottoasrais' is because they see the same way."

"I am sure there is a perfectly good reason your dad hasn't told you yet. It probably has something to do with your coming of age ritual," Camille comforted her.

"So where are we going and how long till we get there?" Digger asked.

"I don't know," Gretchen replied.

Julia asked, "What did you think of when you stepped on the blanket and told it to go?"

"I was thinking of Dr. Who and the time and space tubes he travelled through," Gretchen replied honestly.

"That would explain the nothingness around us and the flashing colors," Ethan said with a smile. "I'll take this over those mirror men any day."

"It's been two days and we haven't heard anything from them," Helen cried. "We should have heard something. Ethan has learned to use his whisper-speak nearly perfectly. He would have tried to make contact, I know him."

"Gabriel is bringing Gregory here to assist us with finding them," Atticus reassured her.

Julian walked out of a dark section of the cave with a worried look on his face.

"What is it that troubles you, my friend?" Luis asked.

"Chief Nico does not think they are coming back and it does not bother him," Julian replied.

"If he did anything to harm my son, I will..." Atticus began ominously.

"Give me five minutes with him and I will find out if he knows anything," Luis interrupted.

"The gods themselves will not be able to help him, but we will not be the judge and jury." Gregory's sonorous voice echoed throughout the cavern as he and Gabriel materialized. "Allow the elders their punishment if harm has befallen our children."

CHAPTER TWENTY THREE

WATER UNDER THE BRIDGE

66 **A**lright Gretchen, let's try this again," Camille encouraged. "I understand it is hard to find the mountain and caves that our friends call home but this blanket is not nearly as spacious as the Tardis."

"You need to relax and think of a place that you would like to be," Julia suggested. "Think of a place that would help you relax."

Digger and Ethan sat on the blanket watching the movements of the world around them.

"It's pretty cool that there really are multiple dimensions and ways to visit them, like the Serenity Channel," Ethan mused.

Camille looked at him with aggravation. She silently decided that if he didn't stop talking she was going to have to push him off the blanket.

"Good topic Ethan, but I nor anyone else here has experience in being a time lord, so until we find a way out of here please leave the Discovery channel comments alone!"

Gretchen tried to think of a place somewhere nearby. But since they went through the tunnels to the University she couldn't picture the area. She definitely didn't want to go back to Lexington. Gretchen remembered sitting on her bed with friends talking about school and stuff. She could see a post card on her mirror of a place she always wanted to go.

Seconds later they were on the ground, sort of. They had landed on some rocks in a river near a massive water fall. The sun was coming up and mists glinted where the falls crashed into the river.

"We are back, on the ground and in our dimension, I think," Digger yelled.

"Yes, it is our dimension," Ivy said "but where are we?"

Camille and Ethan turned to Gretchen.

"Niagara Falls!" Camille announced. "Really, you were thinking of the postcard on your mirror."

"Yeah, you said think of someplace that I could focus on near where we were. Niagara

Falls is somewhere that I always wanted to go and I saw the postcard that my dad got me last time he was up here working," Gretchen explained.

"Just so you know, we are nowhere near the Virginia mountains," Ivy pointed out. "You are going to have to work on your geography now that you know you are a Jinn."

They all laughed except Julia who was drooped over on the blanket.

"Oh no, the sun is coming up and we are in the middle of the river," Ivy cried. "We need to get her out of the sun, like now!"

Ethan looked at Digger and asked, "You got them?"

Digger replied, "We are good, you take Julia quickly."

Ethan lifted Julia and the blanket onto his shoulders and leaped from one set of rocks to the other. Once on shore, the only shelter he spotted was a bridge a half mile away. He ran with Julia's limp body. The old wooden bridge apparently had not been used for many years and planks were missing. He gently placed her underneath and shrouded her with the blanket to block the light.

Digger, Ivy, Gretchen and Camille arrived

a short time later to find Ethan holding the blanket over her tightly.

"Her pulse is extremely weak," Ethan said, concerned.

Digger immediately began to dig a deep hole next to Julia.

"What are you doing?" Camille demanded. "She's not dead! We can save her, somehow."

Ethan considered carefully. He knew one way to save her, but there would be consequences. He stepped towards Julia, hands outstretched, when Digger interrupted.

"The hole is to save her. We need to get her into the hole and NO light can touch her," Digger instructed.

They moved her carefully into the hole, which was impressively deep for being dug by hand and in 10 minutes.

"We need water now, lots of water," Digger exclaimed.

"There is lots of water over there but we have no way to carry it," Gretchen said.

"If you knew how to use your Jinn gift then you could move the water with air," Ivy offered.

"Well I obviously don't know how to do

that. I am sorry, really sorry," Gretchen said, panicking.

"Here's what we are going to do," Ethan decided. "Take off your shoes and any clothes that can hold or absorb water. Fill them up and bring them back to Digger to apply or whatever."

Ivy had her shoes and clothes off down to her undergarments first, followed by Ethan then Camille and Gretchen.

"First time I have ever taken my clothes off to get them wet," Camille commented wryly as she helped Gretchen saturate her top.

"If Jeremy were here, he could have moved the water," Gretchen added sadly.

Digger dumped the water they brought onto Julia, quickly filling the hole. After the third trip they heard a small gasp. They filled up their shoes with water one more time and laid their clothes out on the sunny side of the hill by the bridge.

"She'll be alright," Digger announced.

"How did you know to fill up our shoes and saturate our clothes with water to tote it back and forth?" Camille asked Ethan, impressed.

"I guess it is part of the survival skills that I have to know for my coming of age ritual," Ethan explained. "I am just glad that no one had sandals on and that everyone was wearing underwear."

They laughed and sprawled on the sunny grass in their underwear to dry off.

"That was brilliant," Ivy agreed. "I can't wait to tell everyone how the son of the vampire that killed Chief Nico's brother saved Queen Jasmine's daughter. I will make you a legend, Ethan." Ivy added.

"How about we just leave it at we did it together?" Ethan said, embarrassed.

"You were amazing also," Ivy told Digger. "I don't usually see you in action unless of course you are tunneling through the mountain."

"So why did you have to put water all over her body?" Gretchen asked.

Digger explained that the Grottoasrais' moved from the oceans and lakes to the mountains to avoid being used as bait. They were captured by pirates and used to lure men to a watery death so they could steal their riches. Some of them were used as sex slaves and controlled by their masters to perform hideous acts with anything that paid.

"I thought that you couldn't capture an Asrais? They are supposed to be brutally violent if restrained," Gretchen asked.

"The scarf of Kale neutralizes them," Ivy explained.

"So Julia was starting to dry out in the sun light and you had to rehydrate her before she lost all her water?" Ethan asked.

"Pretty much," Digger replied. "That is why they stay in the moist parts of the caverns and caves until dusk. The moist night air and the occasional splash in a pond or lake is all they need."

"We have a pretty good relationship with them," Digger added. "Occasionally the Chief gets into it with the Queen over certain things. Ivy and my mom usually work it out and bring peace back to the clan and tribe, right Ivy?" Digger asked.

When she didn't respond, they looked around.

"Up there," Gretchen shouted. "Ivy is at the top of the hill and she is on the phone."

"Phone," Camille cried, "where did she get a phone? Ivy don't call, stop!"

It was too late. Ivy had already dialed and was waiting for an answer on the other end of the line.

"What is that?" Helen sensed a vibration from the top of the cave. "Shhh, it's a phone on vibrate," she said, perplexed. "No one is to have a phone here."

Julian agreed. "Our people have no need for them, so we banned them."

"I hear sounds on the other side of that rock face, around 100 feet up," Helen said.

"Luis, cover me," Julian instructed. "It might be one of those mirror men."

"I've got your six, brother. I am right behind you," Luis stated.

They moved as if dodging bullets up the side of the cavern, swinging and climbing from stone outcroppings. When they reached the top, Julian swung around a stalagmite and into a passageway to the surface. A familiar figure paced the rocky floor, cell phone in hand.

"Hello little one," Chief Nico said into the handset.

"Hi sir, we really need your help," Ivy replied. "Did the others get back alright last night?" she asked.

"Yes, they are fine. Are all of you still alive, I mean alright?" the Chief asked.

"Well sort of, but we are lost," Ivy admitted.

"Ivy put the phone down, hang up now,"

Camille screamed, running frantically towards her.

"It's OK! The Chief gave me the phone before we left just in case we were in trouble," Ivy yelled back.

"What kind of traitorous behavior is this, my Chief?" Julian demanded. He restrained the Chief while Luis ripped the phone from his hands, breaking all of his fingers in the process.

The Chief shrieks echoed throughout the miles of caverns and tunnels.

"You Blackguard," Julian cried out in contempt. "How I could have truly been so blind to your hatred of Lord Atticus and Luis," Julian bellowed. "You have spread so much rhetoric over the years concerning them that you are consumed by blind hatred and revenge. I should..."

"No Daddy, don't," Ivy called out from the other end of the phone.

Julian had forgotten that Ivy was out there and needed him. Luis turned the phone on speaker as they clambered down the cave walls with Chief Nico in grasp.

"What is it?" Aurora asked as Julian and Luis got closer with the Chief.

"His blind hatred has laid question to his

judgment," Julian growled as he threw the Chief to the ground. Luis placed a foot upon him, pinning him to the floor.

Camille had led Ivy back down the hill where the signal was not quite as good but at least they were out of sight.

"Mama, is that you?" Ivy cried.

"Yes, love we are here. Are all of you alright?" Aurora asked.

Ivy decided not to worry her mother by telling her about Julia. "We are good, I was just calling Chief Nico like he told me to if we needed any help," she explained. "I guess I wasn't thinking about the mirror men kids. I am sorry, that's what you are all upset about, isn't it?"

Ivy dropped her head as she looked at Camille, Gretchen, Ethan and Digger sitting half naked on the side of the hill.

"Ok baby, it is not your fault," Julian assured his only daughter. "Do you know where you are? It has been three days and we were worried."

The kids looked at each other in confusion, wondering where the three days went.

"We were in a time tunnel," Camille explained. "Gretchen needs a little more training with her gifts. We are now at Niagara Falls."

"That certainly explains why we were not able to contact you these past few days," Helen replied.

"Yes Madame, we were going to try and contact you after we took care of Julia and put our clothes back on," Camille said, flustered.

"What happened to Julia?" Aurora asked, alarmed. "Is she alright?"

"Yes, she is resting now. We arrived here at dawn and well, she started to dry up," Camille said. "Digger and Ethan were amazing and she is resting in a little cave that Digger built. We used our clothes and shoes to gather water to apply to her skin, and it worked. That's why we don't have clothes on."

"Have you encountered any mirror men?" Helen asked.

"No, I mean not that we have noticed," Ethan replied. "I am thinking that using this phone has probably compromised us."

"You are right Ethan, we probably don't need to talk any longer on the phone," his mother agreed. "Get that phone as far away from you as possible. Make them work to track you down. We are going to devise a plan on our end to get you home safely."

"I know you will, Mom. Tell Dad that I love him and I will see him soon. We can keep in contact though the air," Ethan replied.

"Madame, have you told my father yet?" Camille asked.

"Oh yes my dear. He is here in the mountain with us working with Lord Atticus, Mr. Anthony and Gabriel. I know that he will contact you as soon as he hears the news that you were found."

"We are going to have to stay put until it is safe to move Julia this evening," Gretchen replied. "Did you all know I was a Jinn? I guess that is a stupid question; I suppose my dad is one too," Gretchen added.

The silence on the other end of the phone was the only answer Gretchen expected.

Ethan had been thinking of how he was going to get rid of the phone as to mislead the mirror men. "I am going to tie the phone on a broken piece of the wooden bridge and let it float down the river."

"Great idea," said Digger. They walked back to the bridge to gather materials.

"I am so sorry," Ivy apologized as they lay on the warm grass on the side of the hill.

"It is not your fault. You were a pawn for a man that has wasted too much time on revenge at whatever price," Camille reassured her.

"What is all the fuss?" Atticus asked as he returned with Gregory and Anthony.

"The kids, they are OK, well sort of OK," Helen explained as she hugged Atticus.

Atticus saw Chief Nico lying on the ground.

"I suppose that he has something to do with the racket," Atticus commented dryly.

Aurora quickly filled them in on the events of the last hour.

"Are you honestly that much of a scoundrel that you would take revenge on me through my son and your families' children?" Atticus was beginning to lose his temper.

"He isn't worth it, Atticus. The elders will deal him his punishment." Gregory placed his hand on his friend's shoulder. "We need to focus on the children and get them home quickly and safely, now."

"You can't. The elders won't let you interfere in the mission now that the mirror men know where they are," Nico stated smugly. "I turned on the phone that I gave to little Ivy just as she left the tunnels. As soon as they hit the surface they were being tracked."

"I still don't understand why you have so much hate in your heart for Lord Atticus," Julian asked his Chief.

"Lord Atticus? He was no Lord when he killed my brother," Nico replied angrily from his prone position. "He only received the title of Lord after the families chose to walk in the light. Now that he is the only living vampire of royalty he becomes Lord of the Vampires, the mogul of clean energy, the last of his kind.

"That is until he petitioned the witches to assist him and his wives to grant him an heir. Just like he killed my brother, he killed his wives as they tried unsuccessfully to bear him a child. Then she comes along, a half breed whose mother was nothing but a cleaning woman for the witch coven. She begged the high priests to perform the magic mating ritual using the Mandragra root. Only a fool would make such a sacrifice for a child that is unborn."

"What Atticus and Helen did was for the greater good of us all," Gregory admonished Nico. "Yes, the price was heavy, but that was their choice, a choice to fulfill the writings of the Savant and bring honor to our kind."

"Savant, really, if they were still around

they would deal with killers like Atticus with death," Nico replied.

"You never listened to Atticus' side because you were so sure that Jose could not lie to you. The truth is, Jose lied to you about everything all the time, you foolish bore," Gregory snapped.

"Nothing can or should bring your arrogant brother back," Atticus declared. "He was a fool who met his just fate sooner rather than later. The night he died, Jose was so consumed with hatred that he blocked all the entrances to the little cave we sheltered in. When Victoria and I returned from a late night walk down to the river, he was lying in wait," Atticus explained. "He threw large stones at us and prevented us from entering. As the sun began to crest the mountain top, Victoria became weaker.

"When I tried to shelter her, Jose launched larger stones at us forcing us to move again and again. Finally, even with all my strength and power, his assault became too much for me. I collapsed on the ground, unable to give her any further protection. Your brother watched as Victoria's body shriveled on the ground below.

"In pain and anger, I mustered enough

strength to stand. I told him that he was a fool. He came at me with a rock the size of a small car. To protect myself I raged upon him, taking a piece of his throat out before he could release the rock. As he lay dying, I told him what Victoria had shared on our walk. She had decided to accept Jose's hand in marriage."

Chief Nico went silent and motionless, considering Atticus' story. "You are the liar," Nico decided. "All of you have been manipulated by Atticus' charm and wealth. He killed Victoria because she refused his hand in marriage. Jose tried to stop him but Atticus was all doped up on fresh blood and attacked him as Victoria lay dying. Yes, I am sure that is the truth of it. Don't listen to this silver-tongued royal vampire; he thinks nothing of us poor mountain dwellers."

Atticus turned and walked away.

"I have heard enough from this old fool," Aurora said flatly. "Julian, you are the deputy. Deal with him before I allow Luis, Atticus or Helen do so."

"That won't be necessary." Gabriel appeared and lifted Nico to his feet. "Lord Bashshar, the elders and the very real Savants are going to mete out his punishment.

"However, Nico was correct when he said that you cannot physically assist them back. They will and must have contact with the mirror men. I have seen our children in action and I have as much confidence as do the elders in their safe return."

Nico laughed, "I told you, there is nothing you can do. You are going to lose everything now Atticus, and everyone that you love!"

Atticus turned back to Nico, lunging forward to rip his head off. Gregory stepped quickly between the two. "What you are thinking will not bring Ethan home. Nico is scared and would prefer you to end his life, making him a martyr rather than having to endure the elders' punishment. Do not allow him that satisfaction."

Atticus halted, and then stepped towards Helen. She took his hand to absorb some of his energy.

"I must go now," Gabriel said. "Remember you and the other gifted ones are not to help the children, Atticus. I will explain to the elders that you are staying here until this situation is resolved."

"Thank you my friend," Atticus replied.

They huddled and began discussing possible ways to help their children before the mirror men arrived. But every idea ended up with one of them teleporting or devising a shield for the children until the adults could join them at Niagara Falls. Helpless, they realized their only resource was hope.

CHAPTER TWENTY FOUR

THE CRUX

Camille spoke with the little animals that came to visit and asked them to keep watch; Ethan asked the trees to guard the skies for them. Digger and Ivy stayed barefoot on the ground so they could feel any changes coming.

"I have to be home in two weeks for conditioning training before soccer season starts," Camille blurted out. "I also have a recital in September."

Ivy enjoyed soccer but was not very good at it. Trying to distract her, she asked Camille to teach her some tricks when they got back to their mountain.

"I would be happy to teach you a few moves to improve your skills," Camille agreed. "Now we just need to figure a way home from here. If my calculations are right we are only around 600 miles from your place."

"That's a long way," Ethan replied as he dressed. "Walking is probably not going to be an option especially if we are the prey."

Gretchen was putting her clothes on and said, "It is my fault that we are way up here. I panicked."

"You are not to blame, you didn't even know that you were a Jinn in the first place," Ethan comforted her. "I have seen a lot in the past few years since I found out what we all are. I really had my doubts about some mythological creatures existing, though, and Genies or Jinns were one of them. Not anymore."

"Yeah if it weren't for you we would all be dead or mirror men zombies by now," Ivy added.

"Let's stay focused on Julia getting ready to move soon," Camille said. "I am certain that our parents are going to contact us soon with a viable option for movement."

"Hey look up there, on the bottom of the bridge," Gretchen shouted.

There was a COTO sig carved into one of the supporting beams. Camille smiled at the thought that a thousand miles from home someone was tagging her original design.

"There isn't much to do here," Ivy sighed to Ethan. "Do you want to skip some stones with me?"

Ethan thought that could be fun for a while. "Sure, but I will warn you I am pretty good at it!"

"Me too," Digger boasted as he followed them down to the river side.

"There must be something we are missing," Senona complained. "Gabriel is always giving us clues on options if we are in dire need, and right now we are in dire need!"

Aurora repeated with near-perfect memory what Gabriel had said. "Remember you and the other gifted ones are not to help the children, Atticus."

"That's it," Helen chirped. "The gifted ones are not to help the children. That does not say that we can't have someone not gifted help them."

"Exactly! I know that Camille would have already made contact with the animals and Ethan has probably communed with the trees. So what we need is a fast animal to guide them out of the area and then bring them home," Senona said excitedly.

"I have heard tell of a Bayard that exists in the mountains of Pennsylvania just shy of the New York state border. That's near the children," Julian suggested.

"I am afraid that may draw more attention than we already have," Atticus replied. "The chance to ride such an amazing horse would be very exciting and thrilling for the children, though."

They continued to brainstorm as Jasmine approached. "What is going on here; why are you talking about the Bayard?"

"We have found the children," Aurora said.

"I do not feel them here," Jasmine replied. "Are they on their way home now?"

"Soon," Helen murmured.

"Where are they and when should we expect them?" Jasmine asked.

A long silence lingered after her question.

"They are in Niagara Falls and they are hiding now, waiting for the sun to set so Julia can travel," Atticus explained. "The crux is that the mirror men know where they are, no thanks to Chief Nico. Due to his actions, he is no longer in charge. Julian is going to accept the position as Chief, as he should have many years ago."

Jasmine paced back and forth, constructing the events in her head.

"I will talk with Chief Nico later about putting my daughter in harm's way. Right now we have to get the children before any harm comes to them," Jasmine said.

"There is only one problem with that," Helen replied. "The elders have advised us not to intervene with this situation."

Jasmine paused. "I am not sure that I can grant that request. We have had very little threat from these mirror men before you came here. Perhaps this visit was not a good idea. What is the worst thing the elders could do to us if we interfered?" Jasmine replied, lowering her eyes.

Gregory spoke softly and confidently. "I realize that at this time this issue is not affecting your children, Jasmine. However there are thousands of other children around the world, including quotidian's, that are being infected daily.

"At this point we still don't know who is behind this invasion and we certainly don't know what their end game is. The fact that they are going after children is reason enough for us to continue on. We need to stay focused on the future and first bring our children home and then find the eminence grise.

"The mirror men are evolving. It will not be long until they find their way into your world, too. We have all been scarred by history, by the times we have ignored a situation because it did not threaten us personally. We have seen how entire cultures and creatures have gone extinct because we were late to put an end to a problem.

"My daughter is out there along with yours. Our children agreed to this journey, but not to write their names in a history book or to be paid for their service. They came on this journey to meet others like themselves, have fun and, if they could, help stop these mirror men to protect their future and ours."

When Gregory finished, Jasmine was nodding her head. She had trust and hope in her daughters, especially Julia. Helen had felt many pairs of eyes and ears listening to Gregory's words. His passionate plea may have been a significant turning point for them all.

"We need to make contact with them and

send them some benign assistants," Jasmine said, resigned. "Niagara Falls is too large an area for anything to find them successfully."

"I bet Camille and Ethan can be contacted in one minute," Max chirped confidently. Many of the children had gathered behind the adults to listen. "Go on sir, talk to Camille. Ms. Helen, talk to Ethan. Go on, do it now!" Max insisted.

"We first need a plan and something solid that we can tell them. We don't need them getting distracted," Senona cautioned.

"Gregory is going to talk with Camille and find out any details that can give us their approximate location," Jasmine explained. "Anthony is going to speak through Helen and Ethan with Gretchen and give her a crash course on how to use her gift to get them home safely. Senona and I are going to use the bats around there to help us find the best departure site for a clear ride home."

"Do you have anything you want to tell Camille?" Gregory asked Max.

Max thought for a minute and said, "Tell her we are all waiting for her and we know that they are going to be home soon."

Senona looked over at Max with a smile; he recognized it as the 'I love you' smile.

CHAPTER TWENTY FIVE

BEST LAID PLANS

"OK Father, I will let everyone know that it won't be long now," Camille replied wordlessly to Gregory. "Tell Max and the others that we miss them too. If we had Jeremy and Talon here we would just start walking and have them crush any mirror men that attacked us."

"Ethan, Ethan!" Camille whispered outside the little cave where she waited with Gretchen and Julia.

"Ivy, Digger!" she whispered a little louder.

Frustrated, she resorted to air speaking with Ethan. "Ethan I am trying to find you. I just spoke with my father."

"We are up here on the big bridge, checking out the falls. You should come over here; it's really cool!" Ethan said.

"Do you think it is safe that you are a mile or so away from us? There could be mirror men watching our every move. You didn't even tell me you were leaving," Camille shot back.

"I don't know what she is worried about. It's not like we are going to get out of here without them finding us anyway," Ethan complained aloud.

"What did you say?" Ivy asked Ethan.

Ethan explained that he and Camille were having an argument in his head, well their heads. "Camille is upset that we left them alone, and that we are so far away."

"Tell her that we were skipping stones and we are sorry and coming back now." Ivy didn't want to cause any more trouble.

"We are heading back and Ivy says she is sorry. I am not as sorry because at least I got to see some of the great Niagara Falls," Ethan told Camille.

"Argh!" Camille said aloud and stomped her foot.

The sun had gone down some and Julia had climbed out of her hole. She stood with Gretchen only a few feet away.

"Is everything alright?" Julia asked, concerned.

"Yes, unfortunately he is fine and on his way back," she sighed.

Ivy, Ethan and Digger stood over the falls for another minute before making the trek back to their hiding spot.

"Hold on to my back," Digger told Ethan. "I will have us back in no time."

Ethan chuckled. "Thanks but don't worry about me!" He leaped off the bridge and bounded back to the path. Digger and Ivy were not far behind.

"It's nice that you got back so fast," Camille told Ethan when they showed up out of breath.

"We weren't followed," Ethan insisted.

As Camille shook her head she felt her father trying to contact her but he wasn't as clear as earlier.

Gregory asked Camille, "We need for you to tell us as much as possible about your surroundings in the day and at dusk."

Camille repeated this to the others. They described how a bit of light from the falls area filtered near them, and the river moved sort of north to east but not too quickly. The mist from the falls was now blowing their way and they could hear a roar but none of them could explain its source.

"That is excellent information, honey. I will share it with the others," Gregory replied.

Ethan was also being contacted by his mother but was having a difficult time communicating between Gretchen and Anthony.

"I am sorry that I haven't told you more as you got older," Anthony explained to Gretchen. "It was so difficult losing your mother. Being a Jinn is like Dr. Jekyll and Mr. Hyde. We sit on the fence between right and wrong. I know it sounds like an excuse, but I wanted you to have a normal childhood before you learned what you are."

Gretchen listened to her dad's words carefully as they came out of Ethan's mouth. She knew that her mother's death had hurt him deeply. Having all that power but still being helpless against cancer must have been agonizing for him.

"Daddy, I am sorry for being difficult sometimes. I guess I understand a little better now. I do need to learn how to use this gift though, and I want you to teach me," Gretchen replied.

"I am going to have to start right now,"

Anthony told Gretchen. "We know that you can get everyone back home. I am going to give you a crash course on using your Jinn gift."

Ethan stopped talking for Anthony as he sensed some disturbance nearby. The trees were shaking violently on the north side of the river. There wasn't a sound in the air but a shrill ringing pierced their ears.

"They are coming," Ethan announced.

"Ethan you must stay focused on Anthony and Gretchen," Helen told him.

Ethan grabbed Gretchen's hand and moved behind the hill. Continuing to speak for Anthony, he said, "Gretchen, you need to gather energy from everything around you including your friends when you are ready to make your flight. You already know that there is magic and energy in everything. We can move by redirecting that energy into the object that you choose for your transportation."

"How do I control where I am going?" Gretchen asked. "That was the hardest part."

"Control is the most difficult part of any gift. Sometimes you won't end up where you want to be, but where you need to be," Anthony replied.

"We are going to send out an energy signal that you will recognize once you are safely out of there," Anthony explained. "Jasmine has received a sonar map from the area bats. She says to leave immediately and run to a vineyard less a mile west of your current location."

Ethan couldn't hold on to the signal any longer as the piercing sound tore through his ears. Camille instructed him to run along the river edge and they would follow.

Ethan raced to the river bank and glanced around to orient himself. Emily, the girl from the park, stood watching him across the water. Startled, he halted and waited for his friends to catch up.

"What are you waiting for?" Ivy screamed. "We have to get to the vineyard."

"We already know that," Gretchen replied.

"You see that girl and boy on the other side of the river?" Ethan asked worriedly.

It wasn't easy for the others to make them out, but two forms were detectable amongst the rocks.

"Yes. So that is another reason for us to keep moving," Ivy insisted.

"That is Emily, the mirror man that I spoke

with in Savannah, I am sure of it," Ethan told them.

"Then it's good that they are on the opposite side of the river," Camille replied.

They took off again, but moments later another group of kids started running towards them. Digger stopped and picked up some stones from the side of the river and began hurling them.

"I have an idea," Julia exclaimed. "When I say so, everyone run up the hill to flank those kids and then keep running. I will catch up."

Agreeing, they waited as Julia stepped into the water and started blowing on it. A fine mist followed by a dense fog began to form and cover the riverbank. Julia signaled them to go. Digger picked up a few stones for good measure as they ran up and around the other kids. Many of them seemed dazed and confused and some were even running into the river. Julia met up with them a few hundred feet ahead, and only a half mile from the vineyard.

"That was interesting," Camille said appreciatively to Julia.

"Interesting?" Ethan asked.

"Yes, although the fog was crazy amazing I don't understand why they were affected by it," Camille said. "I mean, if they are mirror men why didn't they just run through it since they were locked onto a target?"

"Very good question!" A voice rang out over the narrowing river. Emily had followed them on the other side of the river but she was closer now.

"We have been studying you too," Emily admitted. "Those are still young. They still need some downloads as well as additional control, which will come as they learn to let go."

Ethan heard Camille wanting to say, 'So why don't you come over here and deal with us yourself?'

"Why do you have to make this hard on yourselves? What I am saying is that we are here to stay. Nobody has even noticed us for a few years and honestly no one probably cared anyway."

Knowing her already, Ethan decided to respond. "I thought that we already had this conversation. I told you that your leader was a more of terrorist and fiend than a friend."

"Why are you so bitter, Ethan? Maybe you are not as happy as you thought with your friends?" Emily was trying to bait him. "Look what Gretchen has done by not learning how to control her gifts. You all have lost three days and are 600 miles from family. Ivy turned out to be such a little sneak with her tagalong brother, oh yes and little Julia? Yes, if it wasn't for her issue with sunlight, you could have made it closer to home by now.

"I haven't forgotten Camille and her over-compensating to be a leader and strong woman because of her pathetic family issues," Emily continued in her sweet voice. "Then there are your friends that use their gifts for trivial things when they could change the world, really a waste." Emily laughed.

Each of them wanted to cross that river and tear her to shreds, but they didn't. Instead, they focused on the petite girl and her friend listening for any additional details that would help defeat the mirror men as they were instructed.

"Think about how much better your life would be if you could do anything you wanted and on occasion take care of little issues for Mother," Emily suggested. "I don't want to mess with your schedule, but I can offer all of you all a great new life with lots of little extras. Oh, I know your friends and family will miss you for a little while; mine did too. But they will move on; after all, everyone is replaceable."

"We have made a choice to maintain order in the world as who we are and with what we have," Camille declared. "I don't know how little respect you had for your life but we are going to make a difference."

Gretchen knew that they had to go and yanked on Camille's arm. Emily seemed to be processing Camille's words and was silent for a minute.

"As I see it, you have lost this round with us," Camille decided. "You are on that side of the river and we are here and the others are still lost in the fog."

Camille and the others turned to leave. Emily called out, "Not so fast!" She placed her hands on the water and out of nowhere thousands of fish began piling one on top of the other, creating a bridge over the river. Emily and her friend started walking across on the bridge of fish. More mirror men materialized from the trees and followed them across.

"You see, I am not so different than you," Emily said. "I saw a different future that I liked and wanted to be part of it."

"We already told you we don't want your

future. We are going to make our own future," Ethan replied.

"I think you will like ours though. It doesn't hurt and as a matter of fact it could begin with just a kiss," Emily explained.

"Right, and end like those ones, walking around aimlessly in the fog. No thanks," Ethan replied.

"You're a silly boy. Camille knows those ones don't have our gifts but they will do what we ask them," Emily said with a little laugh.

Ethan shook his head and took off running towards the vineyard.

"There, over there!" Ivy cried. "I see the rows of grapes, we are almost there."

Emily and the mirror men were getting closer. Julia handed Gretchen the blanket that she had been wearing as protection from the light. Gretchen placed the blanket near a silo.

"Everyone on the blanket, I only have a minute to get focused and get us out of here," Gretchen cried urgently.

They positioned themselves on the blanket, watching the mirror men approach. Gretchen tried to focus by taking deep breaths in through the nose and out through the mouth.

"Help her," Camille shouted at Ethan.

The mirror men and Emily stopped 40 feet from where they sat exposed and vulnerable on the picnic blanket.

"Why are they not coming any closer?" Ivy asked.

"It's the grapes," Julia replied. "Grapes release a sound through their skin as they grow and expand. It's classic nature – silence and nothingness don't exist. I am guessing that they can hear it but can't process the sound so they consider the grapes a threat."

"Sweet," Ivy replied. "I will have to thank the next grape before I eat it."

Camille saw that Gretchen was wavering in and out, and told everyone to hold on.

"As I told you before, Ethan, just a kiss and I could change your life forever," Emily said calmly.

Ethan ignored her, realizing they were about to make their escape.

"By the way Camille, do you recognize this cute young guy?" Emily asked. A young man stepped from behind the other mirror men and stood beside her. Camille gasped when she saw her friend from the G6.

"Chris, is that you?" Camille shouted.

"Yes, Camille it's me. I met these really cool kids and they are going to make all those dreams I told you about come true," Chris said excitedly.

"Emily, if you or anyone harms him, I will..." Camille warned, not sure if she still had a chance to save him.

"I told you before that we only want to help kids fulfill their dreams, not harm them," Emily replied.

Camille didn't know how much time she had before Gretchen was going to launch this blanket home. She thought that she could still help him if she could convince him to come with them. She would first have to break Emily's grip from his hand.

"No," Ethan told her as he grabbed her arm, "I know what you are thinking and you can't jeopardize everyone here for this one guy."

"I know you're right," Camille replied sadly. "It's hard because I kind of like him a lot, you know, we get each other. I think if I can save him from the mirror men, maybe we could really have something special. I am sorry Ethan!"

As Camille finished her thought she

turned into a ferret, breaking Ethan's grasp and leaping off the blanket just as Gretchen launched into the time warp thing.

"Camille!" Ethan screamed. "What have you done?"

Gretchen was in a kind of trance and seemed calm and confident as they travelled. The rest of them sat wordless and subdued, staring at each other.

"Frogs, toads - that is it," Gretchen announced as they arrived at the pond that the mountain water slide emptied into. The pond was illuminated with the reflection of the moon as little blue and red fairies did their part to assist in the safe arrival of the children. Parents and friends were waiting anxiously for them, hoping that Anthony's signal would be recognizable to his little girl.

Jumping of the blanket first was Gretchen. She embracing her dad, saying "Frogs, toads - you know how much I love listening to them."

Jasmine and her daughters cried and smothered Julia, Julian lifted Digger in one arm and Ivy in the other and Aurora kissed them both, Helen hugged Ethan while Atticus hugged them both. Jonathan beamed with pride at his partner and daughter.

"You never disappoint me son," Atticus told Ethan.

"Where is Camille? I know Camille was with you," Max repeated.

"Camille jumped off the blanket as we left to save that boy that she met on the plane," Ethan explained, bewildered.

Gregory shook his head, as if to say he knew that boy was going to be trouble.

"Is he one of them?" Jeremy asked as he bounced up and down like a prize fighter.

"It was hard to tell. Emily made it seem like he wasn't one yet, but they are evolving and studying us as fast as we are studying them."

"We got to get her before they make her drink the juice or take the evil mirror men pill," Max stated.

"Let's all go to Niagara Falls and show them a garg-vamp duet," Jeremy agreed. "Camille is probably going all X-men Emma Frost on them by now!"

Ethan bumped fists with Jeremy, saying, "Missed you out there. I think that we could have taken them if you were there, too."

"If it wasn't for Gretchen we may have

had to start walking," Ivy laughed. "Thanks girlfriend," Ivy said, looking around for Gretchen. "Where did Gretchen and her dad go?" Ivy asked.

"Back into the battle," Gabriel announced softly. "Wish them luck."

I hope you enjoyed

Children of the Others
Collection™
Book IV

LEAVING
SHADOWS

Coming 2013 Digital Spellbound-Book V

If you would like to have A. Dragonblood come to your school to talk about writing, school book festival for book signing or any other event, have your teacher or media specialist contact us at www.childrenoftheothers.com or

facebook at A. Dragonblood

Twitter at A. Dragonblood

A. Dragonblood Blog -
            adragonblood.wordpress.com

Late Spring 2013

**The story continues with
Digital Spellbound- Book V**

The entire book will be dedicated to discovering the origins and purpose of the mirror men. Where they came from, what they want and why it is going to take everything that The Children of The Others have to stop there march.

The Children of the Others
Collection™

ABOUT THE AUTHOR

A. DRAGONBLOOD is a fiction writer who uses spell-binding flair, respect for diversity, humor, action, creative spookiness, imaginativeness and even everyday reality to create stories of plausible fantasy and ordinary magic for young readers.